"I'm sure it's nothing," Emma said. "But everyone is on edge lately because of recent events and…well, it seemed prudent to make you aware."

"You made the right decision." Dillon pulled a pair of gloves from his pocket as he approached the desk. He lifted the envelope carefully and, using the sharp pewter letter opener, he slit it open and peered inside.

"I think we need to get this to the lab," he said, his voice tight.

"What's wrong?" Emma asked.

He stared at the sheet of white paper, folded with three precise folds so that each crease matched perfectly and the familiar trickle of dread ran up his spine.

Three words. Printed neatly. No signature.

Practice Makes Perfect.

The killer had just made contact with Emma Vale….

***

Dear Reader,

If you've read my first Silhouette Romantic Suspense title, *To Catch a Killer,* then you've already met FBI agent Dillon McIntyre. Wry, cynical yet loyal to a fault, Dillon was an easy character to love. When it came time to write his story, I jumped in with both feet.

Finding that special woman wasn't so simple, as Dillon had discerning tastes and plenty of baggage. Fortunately, I discovered Emma Vale, a sophisticated beauty with a heart of gold, and I knew she was the one. When Emma becomes the target of a killer, it's up to Dillon to keep her safe. Dillon discovers he's not only the man for the job...but the man for Emma, as well.

Switching from contemporary to romantic suspense has been a wonderful foray into the darker places in my mind and it's been entertaining cooking up ways to thrill and chill my readers in this new subgenre.

Hearing from readers is always a joy. Feel free to drop me a line either by snail mail:
P.O. Box 2210, Oakdale, CA 95361; or by email at author@kimberlyvanmeter.com.

Kimberly Van Meter

KIMBERLY VAN METER

Guarding the Socialite

Recycling programs for this product may not exist in your area.

ISBN-13: 978-0-373-27708-7

GUARDING THE SOCIALITE

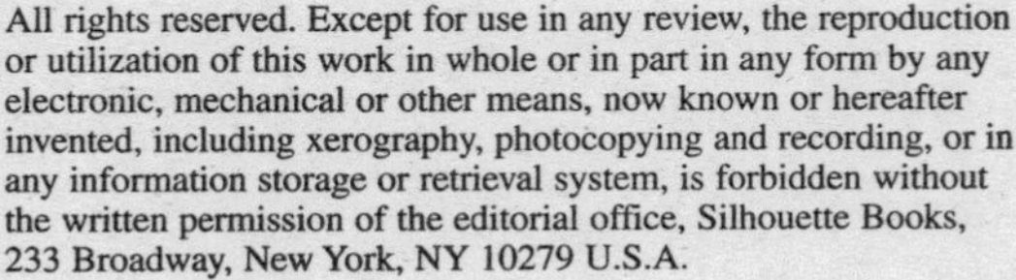

This edition published by arrangement with Harlequin Books S.A.

For questions and comments about the quality of this book please contact us at Customer_eCare@Harlequin.ca.

Visit Silhouette Books at www.eHarlequin.com

Printed in U.S.A.

Books by Kimberly Van Meter

Silhouette Romantic Suspense

To Catch a Killer #1622

Harlequin Superromance

The Truth About Family #1391
**Father Material* #1433
**Return to Emmett's Mill* #1469
A Kiss to Remember #1485
**An Imperfect Match* #1513
**Kids on the Doorstep* #1577
**A Man Worth Loving* #1600
**Trusting the Bodyguard* #1627

*Home in Emmett's Mill

KIMBERLY VAN METER

wrote her first book at sixteen and finally achieved publication in December 2006. She writes for Harlequin Superromance and Silhouette Romantic Suspense.

She and her husband of seventeen years have three children, three cats and always a houseful of friends, family and fun.

Chapter 1

Another dead prostitute.

Special Agent Dillon McIntyre kept his expression neutral but his gut was a roiling mess of bitter resentment that didn't mesh very well with professional civility—not that he was good at playing nice on a normal day. Today it was taking everything he had not to vent his frustration on the woman standing beside him.

Emma Vale—executive director of Iris House—was a right looker, for sure. Too bad not even that motivated him these days. And if it weren't for that damn boss of his, Director Pratt, he'd be sitting in a dark pub somewhere willfully destroying his liver, trying his best to drown out the distant sound stuck in his memory of his former teammate's terrified screaming and the explosion that followed.

Once, he and his partner, Kara Thistle, had been part of the Child Abduction Rapid Development task force within the Bureau. When it involved kids, their team had been considered the big guns. What a change. Today he felt as useful as a water pistol.

A phantom pain ghosted across his face and he caught himself just before he touched the jagged scar that marked his cheek, a gift from his last case.

But no…someone had friends in high places and so, despite his attempts to become completely unreliable, his reputation still managed to impress people.

And therefore, here he was, on a case he didn't want, talking to people he didn't care about.

Ah, bloody hell, that was a poorly constructed lie. Deep down he cared and that was what Pratt had exploited.

He watched dispassionately as she stood beside the locker, her arm curled against her chest with her palm tucked under her chin, staring with moist eyes down at the brunette on the rolling slab, and wondered briefly why she was so obviously heartbroken.

The soft black cashmere sweater molding itself to Ms. Vale's slim and willowy build was in direct contrast to the overprocessed streaks of peroxide-fried chunks of hair that spilled from the prostitute's head, proclaiming without words that the two women had come from different worlds.

Yet, Dillon sensed genuine grief emanating from the tall blonde even as she kept her expression carefully contained.

"Ms. Vale?"

She changed her position, choosing to wrap her arms around herself and jerked a nod to the soft query. "That's her," she said, turning slightly from the body and the coroner's assistant, who was solicitously holding the drape from the woman's face so Emma Vale could provide the identification. She swallowed and took a halting breath as if trying to keep something inside, and he wished for a window into her thoughts. He'd been surprised by the appearance of the executive director herself, figuring an underling would show up to do the unpleasant task.

"Oh, Charlotte," she whispered, closing her eyes briefly.

Dillon motioned to the coroner's assistant and the girl's face disappeared again under the white sheet. "Sorry we had to ask," he said, a modicum of sympathy softening his voice from years of practice. "But she had no family and you were the one listed as an emergency contact."

She didn't waste time on silly chatter and divulged nothing. "Is there anything else you need?" she inquired politely with that clear blue-eyed gaze that Dillon found himself drawn to in the most disconcerting manner and awaited his answer with perfect calm, as if her heartache would have to wait for a more appropriate time. Curiosities that had nothing to do with the case sprang to mind and Dillon had to give himself a mental shake for focus.

"Actually, if you wouldn't mind…I have some questions you may be able to answer." He gestured to the doorway, ushering her from the grisly reminder of her heartache and into the hall.

"Whatever I can do to help," she murmured and dutifully followed, her short heels clicking smartly on the concrete flooring as they left the dour confines of the morgue.

"How well did you know the victim?"

"As well as anyone could, I suppose," she answered.

"Can you be more specific?"

She cocked her head at him in a subtle manner as if to ask *what does it matter* but in spite of this, she answered, "Charlotte came to Iris House about a year ago. She'd been brutalized by her pimp and was terrified for her life. Iris House was her sanctuary." At that her eyes watered but she recovered well. "She was an amazing young woman who didn't deserve to die."

"We're going to do our best to find who did this," he said, the promise tasting stale on his tongue. How many others had he made that promise to? He shook off the pull of bad memories with effort. It'd never been this hard…*before.* It was amazing the sort of damage a traumatic event could do to a person's life. At one time, he'd have jumped at the chance to be on this case.

"Why is the FBI interested in the death of a prostitute? Seems a little beneath the Bureau's notice."

Smart woman. "True, under normal circumstances, though tragic, Ms. Tedrow's untimely death would not have triggered any sort of action on our part but we have reason to believe this was not an isolated case," he answered carefully, doling out only as much information as needed. "Do you recall a woman by the name Darla York?" At her faint head shake, he added, "Actually, you might've known her by her alias, Tiffani Blue." Which, he was pleased to note, elicited more of the reaction he was hoping for.

She frowned, his words clearly triggering a glimpse of something. The words came slowly, as if she were retrieving the memory with difficulty. "A redheaded girl with a gap between her front teeth…she was only with us for a little while." Her delicate mouth tightened, and Dillon could almost see a giant weight land on her shoulders as she said, "I had to let her go. She disregarded the rules of the house. No drugs. It broke my heart to do it but for the sake of the others, I had to. Why do you ask?"

"She's dead."

"Oh, no," Emma exclaimed, her hand going to her mouth. "When? What happened?"

"Her body was found about three months ago, mutilated in the same manner as Ms. Tedrow."

"How awful," she cried. He found it oddly admirable that she cared so much about someone who could've fallen from the face of the planet without anyone's notice. The fact that she was visibly shaken yet held it together with the strength of her will caused his respect level to climb even though he was doing his best to stay detached. Of course, he'd never been any good at that, either.

"Unfortunately, there's more," he informed her, eliciting a wide-eyed, apprehensive stare on her part. He inhaled a short breath before continuing. He hated to add to her burden but there wasn't much he could do about it. "Seems another girl with ties to Iris House was found a few months before Tiffani."

"Who?"

"Her name was Sarah Kuper but she went by the street name of Sweetie."

Emma's shoulders drooped as the name struck a chord. "Sweetie…yes, I remember her. Another one we lost to drugs. She was trying to kick heroin but her pimp liked to keep her doped up, made her easier to handle. In the end, she chose her pimp and drugs over a new life. Oh, God, this is awful…." she said in a horrified whisper.

"When police found Sarah they had no idea that she was, perhaps, the first of many. Pardon my candor but it isn't as if one dead prostitute is going to raise too many eyebrows." She nodded, but she seemed to stiffen and her reaction only served to tease his already-growing curiosity about Ms. Vale. "When Tiffani Blue's body was found, someone sharp over at the local PD noted the similarities between the two and called in the FBI, which is why I'm standing here with you instead of a detective." Well, not the only reason but what was the point of muddying the waters with useless facts about politics and the power of well-heeled connections. Dillon shifted, refocusing as he continued. "The detective thought it looked as if the killer was testing out his method or signature style. By Charlotte, he seems to have perfected it and my gut says we're going to see more."

"More?" Emma tensed as if bracing herself. He didn't blame her. This sort of thing wasn't the easiest to swallow. "More girls tortured like this? What kind of animal…"

"A sexual sadist," he supplied in answer, choosing the frank route rather than dancing around. Something about her manner told him that she'd appreciate his honesty even if she found the information appalling. "We're talking with all the halfway houses and group homes in the area to warn their boarders of the possible threat out there. But there does seem to be a direct connection to Iris House since all of the known victims once stayed there."

She glanced away, her voice bleak. "I know it's too much to hope for that the connection is simply an unfortunate coincidence, but I have to at least ask if that's a possibility."

"It seems unlikely. Of course, it's early in the investigation, but in my experience all signs point to the obvious."

"Of course," she murmured, drawing a shuddering breath. "So what happens now?"

"Well, the Bureau has officially taken over the case so we'll need to talk to your boarders as soon as possible. They may be in danger, but it's also true that one of them may know something that might help the investigation. We also want to take a look at the establishment for security purposes."

"My girls don't trust law enforcement," she said. "What exactly would you be looking for?"

"The basics to start. I'd talk with your staff, take a look around the building, see if there are any vulnerable spots around the property. Then, I'd need to interview the women."

Her regard cooled and he sensed just how protective she

was about her boarders. "I don't want my girls more upset than they already are. They're worried sick about Charlotte. When they find out their worst fears are true, Iris House will be full of grieving women."

"Of course," he said, dropping his voice to affect understanding even though all it would take was a warrant to get what he needed without her consent. But for the moment he didn't see the need to push that hard. He could tell her concern was real as was her fierce determination to shield her "girls." He found that quality…refreshing and yet familiar. Someone else had fought with that kind of intensity for the underdog.

Tana.

Emma caught the minute flinch that was nearly involuntary but she kept her questions to herself and he was grateful. He wiped at the thin sheen of sweat that beaded his hairline and decided to cut the discussion short. "Right. We'll be in touch." He slipped a card into her hand, and then after turning her over to a uniform to conclude the grim business involved with the body, he made his exit.

Emma let out a shaky breath as soon as the tall British man was out of sight. Her nerves were stretched to the breaking point. Grief and guilt sat with equal weight on her shoulders, yet Agent Dillon McIntyre had managed to make her stomach do uncomfortable somersaults with his softly accented voice.

Shame flooded her and she chastised herself with plenty of heat the entire ride back to Iris House. She climbed the stone steps to the 1907 brownstone that became Iris House seven years ago with a large infusion of capital that came primarily from her own trust fund, and Emma allowed the love she felt for this place infuse its strength in her bones for what she had to do next.

The Iris House girls—nicknamed with affection, though they were grown women with the exception of Bella—met her at the door, anxiety and fear marked on their faces.

Chick, her very first boarder, who had, over the years, become her most trusted assistant, stepped forward, her dark eyes reading Emma's heartbreak as easily as if it were scrawled across her forehead with a Sharpie, and her mouth tightened. "Char ain't coming back."

Chick's flat statement cut at Emma but there was no sense in lying. She jerked a nod in sad acknowledgment. "It was her."

Moans followed sharp gasps, and then they all started talking at once, needing answers, shuddering with the realization that it could've been any one of them lying in that morgue, extinguished forever, instead of their housemate. She felt their pain and fear as her own but she had to stay strong even if she was shaking inside. They were depending on her and she wasn't going to let them down.

Emma held up a weary hand. "Girls, please…I'll tell you whatever I know but you have to stop coming at me all at once like a horde," she said, wishing she had more information to give. Chick shushed them all and they headed into the formal living room, where Emma sank into her favorite overstuffed chair and the girls flowed around her like eddies in a stream.

Emma stared into the faces of the women she'd come to love for their various individual quirks and personalities and fervently hoped no one else ended up like Charlotte. Sadly, she hadn't managed to convince all of them to give up their professions, so each night they went out they risked their lives. She drew a deep breath before she began.

"I'm not going to lie, Charlotte died a horrible death. Whoever did this to her…is a monster. And he's out there looking for another victim." She refrained from sharing the connection to Iris House just yet, knowing she'd have to tell them soon enough, but at the moment they had grief to deal with and she didn't want to add panic to the mix. Instead, she said, "We all need to be aware of our surroundings and make sure to communicate with one another for safety purposes. If you're going out, please take a cell phone with you. I'm planning to pick up a few extra cell phones for the house so there are no excuses for not being able to call."

"What are the cops doing to catch this freak?" Evie demanded, earning nods from the other girls. "I mean, don't they have all that fancy computer stuff that can help nail creeps like this? What's it called on those shows… forensics?"

Emma graced the scared redhead with a short smile. "It's not that simple. Forensic evidence takes weeks to sort through and I don't even know if they managed to get anything from Charlotte's body that would help. But I do know that the FBI has gotten involved, so there seems to be something out of the ordinary about her death."

"What do you mean?" Chick narrowed her gaze with suspicion. "What's so unusual about it?"

"Well, it seems that whoever did this to Charlotte may be connected to two other murders…. Do you remember Tiffani and Sweetie?" A few nodded but Chick looked tense. "They're dead, too," Emma finished softly, still reeling herself from the information.

Chick swore and looked away. "Stubborn girl," she muttered angrily, but Emma knew Chick had had a soft spot for the reckless twenty-year-old Tiffani, who'd gotten herself tangled up with a notorious pimp.

Emma and Chick must've been traveling the same road in their minds as Chick said, "Maybe it's that scum licker Mad Johnny that's out slicing girls up."

"I don't know," Emma said, but made a note to mention

it to Agent McIntyre. Speaking of…she drew a deep breath. "There's something else.… Now that the FBI is involved they've assigned an agent to the case. His name is Dillon McIntyre and he'd like to come and talk to you tomorrow. You're not obligated but I think it would be good to be helpful. We all want the same thing and that's to bring justice to this criminal, so I say let's allow the agent to do what he can with our cooperation."

"I hate cops," a small voice said from the group. Emma found the source and withheld a sad sigh. Bella, the youngest of the Iris House boarders stared back at Emma with a hard look in her eyes that shouldn't belong to such an angelic face. Bella was only fifteen but she'd lived a hundred lives in misery before she came to Iris House. She was the only one Emma had had to get special clearance from the state to house, but she'd fought for that clearance because she knew that one more letdown from the system for this kid would be the end of the road. Bella would disappear forever and probably get herself killed before she reached legal age. "I ain't talking to no cops," Bella declared, daring Emma to gainsay her.

"Bella, if you don't want to, you don't have to unless they get a warrant. But we've got nothing to hide and I would like to do whatever we can to help catch this bastard."

Emma rarely used foul language so the momentary slip was enough to give the girls a glimpse of how affected she was by the murders. Bella seemed to settle her hackles but there was an edge to the young girl that outlined her fair features. "Fine. But cops ain't never cared about hookers getting sliced up. Far as they're concerned, it's one less stack of paperwork they gotta deal with."

Emma recognized truth in Bella's contemptuous statement but Emma didn't get that sense from Agent McIntyre. He actually seemed to care even if he was trying not to, which she found odd. She didn't have much experience with FBI agents as a whole, but she imagined that they had to care at some level for the people out there, otherwise why were they in the job?

"Give him a chance, Bella," she said softly, conveying with her tone that not every man carrying a badge was like the man who'd hurt her. Bella looked away then jumped to her feet with a muttered expletive that would've made a sailor blush and disappeared up the stairs.

Chick muttered, "If she slams that door, so help me..." then everyone jumped when that's exactly what happened. Chick sighed and shared a look with Emma, which she waved away.

"Another time," Emma said, not looking forward to another "rules of the house" discussion with the hotheaded teen. She returned her attention to the rest. "So, what do you say? Cooperation or not?"

They were all waiting on Chick, Emma knew. If Chick deemed it all right, they'd grudgingly give in, too. Emma waited. Chick didn't let her down.

"They'd better find who did this," she said finally. "If it helps...I say fine. I just hope it doesn't blow up in our faces somehow."

Emma nodded and agreed. Each woman who stayed at Iris House was given sanctuary with no questions asked. There were only three big rules: no drugs, no bringing anyone home, and each boarder had to hold a regular job. Emma didn't demand that they give up hooking but she tried her damndest to get them to quit on their own. Most of the time, she succeeded. Of the girls currently residing at the house, only two were openly still hitting the streets but Emma was wearing them down. Once the girls realized they could live a different life and started to rebuild their self-esteem and self-worth from the ground up, they discovered they wanted more than the streets could offer.

But other times… Emma tried not to think of the ones she lost.

Like her sister.

Chapter 2

Dillon stared into the mouth of his beer bottle and idly peeled at the label hugging the glass. He ought to feel better. The shrinks had cleared him for duty, not that he'd been itching to get back in the field, but a fellow had to earn a living, right? Except, he'd figured he'd take a desk job somewhere, pushing paper around, not taking on another serial killer case with more lives on the line.

Tana flashed in his memory as he liked to remember her when they were all working on the CARD Team—blond hair tucked into a ponytail, warm green eyes flashing, offering a short, enigmatic smile to one of the many smart-ass remarks that he'd enjoyed trading with his partner Kara Thistle—and he winced. Yeah…he was right as rain.

If only he'd had the stones to tell her how he'd felt. Not that it would've changed anything. She'd still be dead but maybe… No, he shook away the useless direction of those thoughts. He'd be barking mad to allow those thoughts to continue. The shrink had advised him against playing in the field of hypothetical questions. That was one bit of advice he could see the sense in following.

Strip away his unresolved feelings for his former teammate and he was left with another uncomfortable truth. A truth that he dared not admit to anyone but was staring him in the face right now, leering in that knowing fashion that caused him to shake like a small boy caught by the headmaster doing something naughty.

Somewhere among the wreckage of timber and shattered glass of that explosion he suspected was his confidence. And now Pratt had put him front and center at the head of this investigation where women were being carved like Christmas Day turkeys because Emma Vale's daddy had pulled some strings, demanding the best.

So what if the man didn't know the best was actually retired and the second-best was damaged goods? But Pratt had to work with the tools available, and Dillon's worst day on the job was still better than most agents' best, so here he was, without a choice and feeling downright maudlin about the whole thing.

"Bloody hell," he muttered, downing the rest of his beer and rousting himself from the sofa to toss the bottle away. When'd he become such a stupid git? He rubbed at the scar on his cheek and recalled Kara's remark in the hospital as she'd tried to make light of the fact that he'd nearly died, too.

"If it weren't for that prissy accent of yours, you'd look like quite the badass," she'd quipped, though her eyes had watered.

"Don't let the accent fool you," he'd returned with a voice filled with rust and gravel. "I've always been a badass in disguise. Much like 007."

Kara's voice faded as did the smile that formed briefly on

Dillon's face. He glanced longingly at his cell phone, wishing he had the bollocks to just pick up the phone and admit he was having a helluva time shaking off the last case. But his pride wouldn't let him move a muscle. Kara'd likely laugh at him, anyway.

His former partner was living her own life, and he was loath to intrude, so he had no choice but to suck it up and deal, as she'd no doubt say.

He blew out a short breath and wandered to the window to gaze out across the bay. The dark waters glinted with reflected moonlight and he could almost hear the lapping of the waves but for the reinforced glass that walled his apartment. It was a premium place—exorbitantly priced even for the Bay Area market—but Dillon appreciated the quiet peace it offered, especially right now.

His thoughts, blunted by too much beer and not enough sleep, tripped into the space holding his recent encounter with Ms. Emma Vale and blithely tumbled into places he'd never allow himself to go if he were sober. *She was hot,* was the first thing that came to mind, which was quickly followed by the inappropriate, *Wonder what it would take to get into her knickers?*

"Nice, you pervert," he muttered to himself. "Why don't you just lose everything along with your self-respect while you're at it?"

Disgusted by his lack of self-control, even in the privacy of his own mind, he forced himself to focus on something productive.

Grabbing case files from the glass-topped table, he returned to his spot on the sofa and started thumbing through them.

First case, Sweetie, aka Sarah Kuper—the body had been badly decomposed, which hadn't encouraged a real thorough search of the scene where she'd been found, but detectives had managed to get an ID on her from a fingerprint. She'd been bagged and tagged and then stuck unceremoniously in the ground—paid for by the City, of course—when no leads surfaced. Next came Tiffani Blue aka Darla York, a pretty girl with faded red hair and a riot of freckles that made her look younger than her actual age of twenty-one—pervs probably loved the illusion of banging a kid without the penalty of a felony crashing on your buzz. She'd been basically eviscerated.

He blinked, willing himself to sobriety, and refocused. Common cocktail for disaster, he noted as he read her background. Abusive father—started stripping at a young age, which segued to hooking. It was a damn playbook for nearly every sad case walking the streets. They were so easy to select as victims. A dime a dozen, really. No one would miss them and usually, as in the case with Sweetie, no one claimed their bodies as they chilled in the morgue.

Except for Ms. Vale.

She cared. Deeply. The question was why? Not to be a heartless bastard but she was a refined lady, and he could tell from the way she carried herself she didn't grow up on the wrong side of the tracks. He suspected he had that in common with her. He'd grown up with a fair amount of privilege himself as a lad in Hammersmith, London. He could spot a silver spoon upbringing from a mile off, and Ms. Vale wasn't even trying to hide her upscale roots in spite of her penchant for managing a safe house for prostitutes. That in itself made him grudgingly curious as to the why of it, even if he was trying to keep his interest focused on the case.

No…she had an air about her that screamed *wealth* and *privilege.* She'd fit in quite nicely at one his mother's social teas and brunches, he suspected. Lord, he was glad there was an ocean between him and home. If not, his mother—bless her soul—would be dragging him around London to find a wife of some sort, forcing him to choke down biscuits and scones in the presence of some high-bred society girl that bored him to tears. He sighed. Mother may have liked Tana, once she got over the shock of meeting a woman who had a weapon collection that could outfit a small army. Ah, Tana…a world of hurt had awaited anyone who had mistaken the willowy blonde for anything soft and easily pushed around. He missed that woman. Something as horrifying as tears pricked his eyes and he ground them out with a muttered curse.

"Fabulous. I've turned into a country song, crying in my beer like a wanker," he said to the empty room. "Perhaps I should get a hound and a pickup truck and be done with it."

He closed Tiffani's file and sorted through the other folders until he found the one marked Iris House.

He skimmed the contents. Nothing really stood out. The house was purchased seven years ago from the City of San Francisco for a paltry sum as part of a bid to revitalize the historic buildings, and a company named Vale Enterprises had financed the refurbishing. Vale Enterprises—his mouth twitched. Family perhaps? He made a mental note—as far as his soggy brain would allow—to ask Ms. Vale about the connection tomorrow. Likely she'd respond politely yet coolly that it was none of his business, but he was curious nonetheless. Kara was always accusing him of doing things his own way. Well, that much hadn't changed.

He flipped the pages, looking for something that stood out. He found a biography page on Ms. Vale, short and to the point, and completely impersonal. Not that he'd expected all her secrets to be splayed in a nice, neat manner for him but one could hope for small breaks.

Dillon closed the file and tossed it on the pile on the fine leather ottoman before falling back against the cushions of the sofa, his momentary hold on sobriety loosening.

Tomorrow…he was going to crack the first mystery of why a society girl would choose to spend her time running a group home when she was clearly raised to do so much more.

Somehow he couldn't picture Ms. Vale sitting through a tedious dinner while her guests prattled on endlessly. He could only imagine the conversation around the table with her boarders, full of ribald humor, probably enough to curl her straight, fine locks that fell to her shoulders in a fall of honey… Oh bollocks. He was turning into damn William Wordsworth, waxing on about the color of her hair.

He needed to get it together. He needed to blow this case apart and put that sick bastard away.

But at the moment…he needed to bloody well pass out.

Emma was waist-deep in a conversation with Bella's probation officer—and losing ground—when Chick showed Agent McIntyre into her office. She didn't have time to lament Chick's choice of ushering him straight in instead of having him wait in the foyer for she was fighting a battle over Bella.

"I understand completely your predicament. All I'm asking for is a short reprieve. She's been through a lot lately and I'm sure Bella is simply acting out inappropriately due to grief and stress." She refused to look at the agent, afraid her stomach might do that odd flippity-flip that it'd done at their first meeting, and she needed her wits firmly in focus if she were going to keep Bella from being ripped out of her care and returned to a foster home for her latest stunt.

"The girl is a loose cannon and she's dangerous," the probation officer stated, his voice devoid of any hint of warmth, not that Emma was surprised. Bella had once kicked the man in the balls during an altercation at the detention center and he hadn't forgotten. Emma had tried to get a different probation officer due to their history, but the system was overloaded and no one was willing to take on a case like Bella's if they didn't have to. "This latest incident proves she isn't doing well in your care."

"No," she returned evenly, her own hackles rising. "She was doing quite well until a house member recently died. You, with all your experience, should recognize that she's clearly acting out but it will pass. The worst thing we could do is uproot her at this time."

He grunted something in answer that may have been a grudging agreement and Emma took advantage of that small break. "We have a counselor on retainer, and in her last report she stated Bella was making wonderful progress. I assume you've read the report?"

"I glanced at it," he said, which told Emma he'd completely ignored the file but wouldn't admit to it. "But you're missing the point. She punched a man in the face today. That's felony assault."

"And from what Bella said, the man had grabbed her inappropriately. Sounds like self-defense to me."

"Yeah, she would say that," he grumbled, and Emma's hand curled into a fist until she made a conscious effort to relax. She didn't need to get riled up and lose her cool over this, especially while Agent McIntyre was watching and listening. She caught his faintly quizzical expression and she nearly winced. "I'm afraid if you take her from Iris House she will regress—"

"Listen, Ms. Vale, here's the deal. You have temporary guardianship that can be revoked at any time if it seems this experimental program is failing. We have to go with what works and obviously this isn't working as well as we would've liked. Frankly, she belongs in a mental institution with very thick bars." The last part was muttered and likely said before he could stop himself but the momentary slip gave her the ammunition she needed.

"If you take Bella from Iris House I will have no choice but to speak to your superiors about your bias against this young girl. You're looking for a reason to put her away instead of trying to help her. You're not the only one who keeps *files*, Mr. Lufty." She let that sink in for a moment and then said in the nicest tone possible, "I appreciate our little chats. It's nice to know someone cares about our Bella as much as you do. I will have a talk with Bella about her actions today so we can all work toward putting this unfortunate incident behind us. Good day, Mr. Lufty."

She carefully replaced the phone and took a minute to collect herself then presented a calm and pleasant expression to the agent, if only to hide the turmoil making mincemeat of her nerves. She stood and extended a hand. "A pleasure to see you again, Agent McIntyre. I apologize for the wait," she said, gesturing to the chair across her desk.

He regarded her closely, his eyes dancing with a light that bordered on intrigued and impressed as he said, "No worries. Sounds like you have your hands full with someone in your care. She's lucky to have you on her side."

Bella was more than a handful, she wanted to quip but didn't. Bella was a private person and wouldn't appreciate it if Emma shared details. "Yes, well, comes with the job," was all she said and then folded her arms in front of her. "Where should we start? A tour, perhaps? Some of the girls have agreed to talk to you but a few have declined for obvious reasons."

"Obvious?" he repeated.

She cleared her throat and gave him an apologetic look. "It's not personal. Some are uncomfortable with law enforcement as you may imagine. Some have not had the best experiences with police."

"Ah, right. But I'm not a cop so they can rest easy," he said with a grin that was incredibly charming, but Emma resisted offering a reaction. Noting her lack of appreciation for his attempt at softening her, he narrowed his gaze then said, "A tour would be a good start, I suppose."

"Fabulous," she said, rising. "If you'll follow me."

"Lead the way." He paused as she moved past him. "So, according to the information I have on Iris House, it was built in 1907."

"Yes, shortly after the 1906 earthquake that nearly destroyed the city. It's one of the few brownstones in San Francisco. As you probably know, most of the architecture is Victorian." She took a subtle breath in the hopes of steadying her nerves, wishing she could unlock the reason why the agent made her hands flutter and her mind race with things she'd put on a shelf a long time ago in her single-minded pursuit of making Iris House a success. In the seven years since she'd purchased the building she had gone on perhaps three dates. Not that she was looking to date Agent McIntyre—God, no, how inappropriate—but he was a handsome man and he stirred a hunger she'd long forgotten.

It wasn't that she *couldn't* date—for heaven's sake she wasn't a nun—but dating came with complications she had no desire to deal with simply for companionship. It was easier this way—unencumbered—but it was lonely at times and standing close to the first man who stirred anything more than casual appreciation made her nervous.

"The first level as you see is what we like to call the business level of Iris House. The second is the living quarters for the girls and the top is my personal apartment," she said, leading him to the back where a small enclosed garden was hidden. "This is our personal oasis. We plant fresh herbs like thyme and basil in planter boxes. It's very cathartic for the girls and it makes everything smell nice."

"Perhaps I need to garden more often," he quipped, though there was a darkness to his tone that perplexed her. Before she could question him on it, his expression became a neutral slate. "May I see Charlotte's room?" he asked, surprising her with his abrupt request.

"Of course." She looked away, pausing as a ripple of grief flowed through her. She'd avoided cleaning it out, putting it off until she could enter the room without her eyes welling with tears. "What do you hope to find? Perhaps I can help?"

"I'm just trying to get a snapshot of Charlotte as a person. Might help me get an idea of what kind of victim the killer is looking for."

She winced. It was too much of a reminder that Charlotte had been murdered by some psychotic maniac that was still out there. "Of course," she murmured. "Follow me."

They walked up the stairs to the second level and as soon as they hit the landing, doors to individual rooms opened and the women started appearing, some wearing openly hostile expressions and others appraising the agent with experienced eyes. "Good morning, ladies," he offered solicitously, but he received little in response, not even from the ones who looked happy to show him a good time. Emma suppressed a smile and a grimace. Her girls were a tough crowd. Oh, well. The agent's success didn't rely on the approval of the Iris House ladies. Thank goodness. Before Bella disappeared into her room, she'd worn a look of such scathing contempt that it would've doomed him from the start.

"I see what you mean about the unfriendly part," he remarked, unfazed by the cold reception.

"I never said they were unfriendly," she corrected him. "I said some of my girls were uncomfortable around law enforcement. You have to understand the place they're coming from. Many have very few good memories of police. Or men. But this is a place of healing and sanctuary and it's very generous of them to allow you in their space, given their feelings."

He listened and nodded but didn't comment further. She wondered if he was offended, but since he didn't offer any insight to his thoughts, she let it go. She opened the door. "Here it is," she said, swallowing the lump that had risen sharply in her throat. Charlotte's favorite perfume—Love's Baby Soft—permeated the small room as the young woman had practically bathed in it each day. It was one of the other boarders' biggest complaints about Charlotte but now that she was gone it seemed a small thing.

Dillon took one step inside and promptly sneezed. She chuckled softly. "Bless you," she added, then explained. "It was her favorite perfume. Takes a little getting used to."

"Right," he said, wiping at his nose. "It's very…uh, potent."

Emma resisted sharing more. The fact was she was seeing Charlotte as she'd seen her last, chattering about the classes she was going to take at the junior college, excited about a future she wasn't going to have. She'd had high hopes for Charlotte. She'd been so close to getting her off the streets, but Charlotte hadn't managed to sever ties with Mad Johnny, much to Emma's consternation. The memory served to remind her to mention the hot-tempered pimp to the agent. "There is someone you might want to question, Agent McIntyre," she began. He looked up from his search, interest in his yes. "He's a pimp and a mean one. He had an obsession with Charlotte. His name was Mad Johnny."

"Mad Johnny? His mother must've hated him," he quipped, earning a small smile for his effort, but he sobered quickly when he realized she wasn't in the mood for laughs. "You don't by any chance have a real name for him?" he asked.

"No, I'm sorry, but I'm sure the police have him on file. He has a record and a reputation for beating his girls."

"Did he ever come around here?"

"No," she answered firmly. "Charlotte knew the house rules and wouldn't break them, not when she was so close to getting out of that lifestyle." She pushed at the wave of sadness threatening to ruin her calm facade and lifted her chin. "Charlotte loved living at Iris House. We were her only family."

"That seems to be a commonality with your boarders," he mused and she couldn't deny it.

"Their biological families threw them away a long time ago. We're here to pick up the pieces so they can start fresh."

"Why do you allow them to continue prostituting? It's against the law and you know what they're doing when they go out at night."

She walked a fine line with law enforcement. They knew she was trying to help these ladies so they gave her some latitude, but she didn't know this agent or his philosophies and wasn't about to divulge any more than was required. "I actively encourage the girls to quit," she said. "What they do outside of these walls is not my business. The only rule is that they don't bring it home. As I said previously, Iris House is a sanctuary. And I keep it that way."

"So why do you care so much?" he asked, throwing her with his sudden question.

"Why wouldn't I care? They're human beings, too, with hopes and dreams, aspirations, heartaches…just like you and me."

"Some are cons and criminals," he countered evenly.

"Some," she conceded then added coolly. "But mine are

not." He seemed to catch that she'd just circled the wagons and simply nodded. She offered a small smile but it was strained around the edges. Being in Charlotte's space was harder than she imagined. Boarders came and went but she'd never lost one to violence—at least, that's what she'd thought. She suppressed a shiver and inquired, "Are we finished here?"

He shoved his hands in navy blue slacks and did a slow perusal of the mostly pink room but paused at a picture taped to the dresser mirror. He gestured. "May I?"

She hesitated but then realized no one would care what happened to Charlotte's personal effects except her and relented. He plucked the picture from the mirror. "Something tells me this isn't Mad Johnny," he said.

Emma leaned forward for a better look. In the picture Charlotte was smiling beside a well-dressed man, her arms looped around his middle in a way that was very familiar. She frowned slightly. "No. That's Robert Gavin, a very generous man who has donated frequently to Iris House."

"Were he and Charlotte close?"

She drew back, her frown deepening. "No…not that I'm aware," she said, trying to remember if Charlotte had mentioned a friendship with Robert. She couldn't recall, but she wasn't privy to every aspect of her boarders' lives. She shrugged. "The girls are free to befriend whomever they choose."

"Was he…a client?" he asked.

To that she balked. "Absolutely not. Robert Gavin is not that kind of man. His generosity comes from his heart, not from some kind of expectation of sexual favors."

The cynical expression in the agent's eyes made her feel as if she'd just said something incredibly naive, but she refused to feel defensive about her protestation. She knew Robert and he wasn't a bad man. "Mad Johnny was a threat. I'd start there, Agent McIntyre. Are we through here?" She didn't wait for his agreement, as she turned and exited the room. He took the hint and followed. As soon as the door closed, she released a pent-up breath and faced him, refusing to be charmed by the wayward fall of hair that was just this side of unprofessional and likely drove his superiors nuts. "Is there anything else you require, Agent McIntyre?" she asked with as much professional courtesy as she could muster under the circumstances. But the way he cocked his head to the side and openly assessed her made her shiver, and she had to snap her mouth shut for fear of emitting a breathless gasp.

Lord, was she losing her mind? The stress was making her react inappropriately. At least she hoped that was the reason she practically melted every time she looked at him. He was here to do a job and she wanted to help him in any way possible that was professional and appropriate.

Still...*those dark eyes*...they were a killer unto themselves, and she'd be a liar if she didn't at least acknowledge the fact that when he settled that stare on her even the fine silk of her bra felt rough and constricting.

She turned abruptly, anxious to get away and put an end to the disconcerting noise inside her head before she said or did something completely out of character and humiliated herself. "Chick will see you out, Agent McIntyre. Duty calls and Iris House never sleeps."

And thank God for that, she said to herself as she made her escape.

She needed the distraction.

Chapter 3

"Is there anything else you require?"

The agent side of his brain received the question and immediately lobbed it to the reckless, panting fanny hound that was currently salivating at the multitude of sinful ideas happily being tossed about. Thankfully, it was the agent that responded, halting Emma's retreat.

"Actually, is there a place where I could speak to your boarders?" he asked, his tone all business by the grace of God. She didn't look happy about it. In fact, she might've been more pleased if he'd just asked if he could urinate in her herb garden, but she nodded stiffly and knocked on one of the doors in the hallway.

A woman with close-cropped black hair poked her head out, a short glance came his way while Emma talked. The woman nodded but her mouth was a tight slash of compressed lips that spoke volumes.

He rubbed at his forehead. "Nice to be so loved and admired," he said under his breath as Emma returned.

"Chick will bring the girls who are willing to talk with you down in the garden outside."

He refrained from commenting on the unusual moniker until they were out of earshot and heading down the stairs.

"Tell me there's a story behind Chick," he said, pulling his gaze from the gentle sway of her backside with great effort. The woman could stop traffic with that bum. He was thankful she hadn't turned around to answer otherwise she might've caught him staring.

"Story? What makes you think there's a story?" she asked mildly, returning them to the garden, the fresh scent of growing things teasing his nostrils and causing his stomach to twist with hunger. He followed her to the small glass table in the corner near a stone fountain that gurgled soothingly. She took a seat and gestured for him to do the same. When he simply gave her an arched brow, she relented with the tiniest of smiles. "Chick was my first boarder."

"Why didn't she ever leave? Go on to bigger and better things?"

She shrugged. "She finds purpose here. Where else can you spend a day at work and go home feeling as if you've made a difference in someone's life?"

"So she's on the payroll?" he asked.

"Yes. She's my assistant."

"Why didn't you send Chick to identify Charlotte's body? Surely that must've been terrible for you."

"It was awful," she agreed, then met his stare and held it as she said, "But why would it be any less horrible for Chick? She'd known Charlotte as long as I had. Besides, the boarders of Iris House are my responsibility. I don't take that lightly."

He believed her. The fierce flare in her eyes told him that

much and more. Emma Vale was a mystery begging to be uncovered, and he was drawn to that unknown variable in the worst way. Was it because she reminded him so much of Tana? They seemed to share that self-contained quality that hinted at great depth but kept people at a distance with the emotional equivalent of an electric fence. Even their hair color was similar. A shocking question poked at him. Was he attracted to Emma because of Tana? He shook off the fear. They were alike in some ways, but even as much as he'd been taken with Tana, he was feeling something quite different with Emma, which was damn unsettling.

Worse than inappropriate. Worse than ill timed. Just plain…bad.

Emma's chest tightened with the need to breathe freely, but around Agent McIntyre she felt constantly on edge. Law enforcement did not generally rattle her cage, nor was she a badge bunny, prone to salivating at the sight of a uniform. In fact, often quite the opposite was the case as most times her dealings with police were taxing at best. Cops—at least the ones she'd been subjected to in her association with her boarders—were surly, obnoxious and downright rude. Prostitutes represented a mountain of paperwork for very little reward. The judges let them off because there were bigger fish to fry in the city, and the cops ended up feeling ineffectual, which was often a nasty cocktail when handling men hyped up on misplaced machismo. But she knew simply by looking at Dillon McIntyre that he wasn't cut from the same cloth as some of the men she dealt with on an everyday basis. There was a quiet, understated strength that radiated from those dark eyes that was impossible to miss in spite of that lingering flippant sarcasm that saturated his voice when he spoke. And that accent, stubbornly clinging to his inflections, sent a thrill skipping across her pulse points, awakening her senses when that door ought to be shut, locked and perhaps padlocked for good measure.

When had she become such a deep well of bubbling hormones? She gave herself a subtle shake and returned her attention to what he was saying in just the nick of time.

"I have an idea," he said suddenly. "You can call me Dillon and I'll call you Emma," he supplied as if it were the most sensible thing in the world when it most certainly was not. She couldn't imagine that was proper procedure and she hoped her expression echoed that sentiment.

"I don't think that's appropriate," she demurred quietly; just the thought of feeling his name on her tongue felt delicious and sinful. Her gaze surreptitiously drifted to his ring finger and bounced away when she saw it was bereft of a wedding ring. So he wasn't wearing a ring. It meant nothing. Many men, particularly in law enforcement, didn't wear a ring. "I would feel more comfortable keeping the professional lines drawn," she said truthfully. She could only imagine how easy it might be to trip over that line with too much familiarity. Yet, for a moment she allowed herself to savor the idea of such a possibility. Lord, she needed to date more often. This forced moratorium on dating and sex had pickled her brain. Painful as it was, she forced an image of Charlotte back into her mental theater and nearly flinched at the sting. That was better. Best to remember what was at stake. "Agent McIntyre, please tell me you have a suspect in mind? Some clue as to who this person is so you can stop him before he kills again?"

He sobered, the mention of Charlotte serving to douse the teasing light in his eyes. "We're doing our best to catch this person before that happens but that's all I can divulge at this time," he answered, a weight settling heavily around his shoulders that even Emma could see pulling him down. She wondered what caused him to withdraw into himself like that. A previous case? This case? Her curiosity was distracting. As was this overwhelming sense of impropriety that caused her to wonder if he had someone special in his life or if he were a solitary type person, like herself.

She heard the footfalls of Chick and the boarders willing to talk and she rose from her seat. Agent McIntyre followed suit and she smiled for his courtesy. "I'll leave you to your questions," she murmured before taking her leave, brushing past Chick with a quick look of gratitude for her hand in convincing the girls to cooperate.

She wanted whoever killed Charlotte, Sweetie and Tiffani to get his due and if Agent McIntyre could accomplish that, she'd give him every resource she had.

With Emma gone from the room it was much easier to concentrate, which, considering how tough Chick seemed to be with her harsh haircut and equally menacing demeanor, was a good thing.

"What do you want to know?" Chick cut in, wasting no time on chitchat, idle conversation or even pleasant banter.

"What do you know of Robert Gavin?" he said.

She gave him a quizzical look as if to ask *what's your angle* and then answered, "He's a man with soft, girlie hands who's never seen a day of hard work in his life but he has plenty of money and he likes to give some of it to Iris House, so whatever. Why?"

"What do you think of him?"

She shrugged. "He's all right."

"Just all right? Did you know Charlotte had a picture of him on her mirror in her bedroom? To your knowledge were he and Charlotte an item?"

"Char and Robert? Hell no. Maybe there were feelings on Charlotte's side, but everyone knows Robert has had a thing for Emma since the day he laid eyes on her."

Dillon mulled that information over in his mind for a moment. That just made Robert public enemy No. 1 and someone he wanted to get to know better.

"What makes you think that?" he asked.

Chick gave him a look of amusement. "How do you think? When she walks into a room, his eyes are glued to her. He falls all over himself to get a smile from her and then if that wasn't enough I'd say the dinner invitations were the clincher."

"Dinner? Did she accept?"

Chick hesitated, as if suddenly realizing Emma might not appreciate her spilling such personal information, and hit the brakes. "What does that have to do with Charlotte?" she asked, frowning. "Robert Gavin ain't your guy. He's more likely to faint at the sight of blood than to spill it. You feeling me?"

"Deviant people are more adept at hiding their true nature," he supplied mildly then shrugged. "But you may be right. I'm just curious as to his association with Charlotte."

Mollified but still wary, Chick admitted, "I don't know what Char was doing with Robert. Maybe you ought to ask him."

At that Dillon smiled. "Oh, I plan to," he assured her. It could be nothing and this Gavin character could be exactly as Chick described but Dillon had a niggling sense that there was more to Charlotte's relationship with the man than Emma or Chick seemed to be aware of. And that made the man just this side of suspect.

Later that night as Emma sat among a handful of collected photographs of Charlotte that she'd gathered for the memorial, a soft knock at the door made her glance at the clock and wonder who was still awake at this wretched hour.

It was Bella. She opened the door wider and allowed the

teen to enter. "What's wrong?" she asked, worry in her voice. She couldn't help scanning the teenager's thin frame for signs of abuse. Bella had often cut herself before she came to Iris House and Emma worried that she might turn to the destructive habit during times of extreme stress.

Bella tightened her arms around her sides but didn't answer right away. Although Bella knew a lot about things she never should've known, in many ways she was still a frightened girl who needed guidance. It was that vulnerable side that called to Emma. Her hand curled softly as she resisted pushing the errant strand of hair from the girl's eyes. Bella didn't like to be touched, not even with kindness. Not yet. Emma was still working on that broken aspect of the teen's psyche with countless hours of therapy.

Bella chewed the side of her lip, clearly wrestling with something but unsure how to coax it free from her own mouth. Emma smiled and gestured. "Why don't you come and help me with the photos I've put aside for Charlotte's memorial. I could use a second opinion."

Bella nodded and followed, taking a seat on the edge of the sofa to peer at the photos spread across the end table. She fingered a few, pushed aside others and finally picked one. "This is a good one," she offered with a shrug that was a pathetic attempt at showing that she didn't care when Emma knew for a certainty that she cared deeply. Charlotte's death affected them differently. While Emma felt the weight of responsibility for the woman's death, Bella likely felt true grief, which was something she was emotionally ill-equipped to handle.

"I didn't talk to that FBI agent," she admitted in a tight, defensive voice, her gaze cutting to Emma for her reaction.

"That's fine," Emma said, her tone carefully neutral while she continued to sift through pictures. She already knew that, thanks to Chick. "I told you it was your choice." She looked up briefly. "There's no judgment, Bella."

Bella nodded but a small crease appeared in her smooth brow. "You're not mad?"

"Of course not. Ursula didn't choose to speak with him, either," she pointed out mildly, returning to the pictures. "But he seems a very nice, professional man. There's no need to be afraid."

"I'm not afraid," Bella scoffed with more vehemence than the declaration warranted for the situation, and Emma knew she'd hit a nerve. She remained silent and Bella seemed to sulk for a moment, dropping the photo in her hand when she realized she was crinkling it. "What if I should've told him something? Something that might matter to the case, you know?"

Emma looked up, faint alarm at the teen's hesitant admission churning the remains of the hastily eaten dinner she'd consumed hours ago. "Such as?" she asked.

Bella shrugged, but Emma thought she saw tears sparkling in her eyes before she skewed her gaze away. "I didn't want to say nothing because I ain't a snitch, but now that Charlotte's dead I figured it's not snitching. I mean, Charlotte was always real nice to me and we had stuff in common so I didn't want to say…"

"What is it, Bella?" Emma prodded gently, but her palms had begun to sweat. Unease squatted in her belly at the possibilities.

Bella looked up and this time there was no hiding the sheen of tears as she said, "Mad Johnny was making Char run drugs again. She tried not to but he caught up to her and he must've had something on her because she was real upset about it. He was gonna make her hook again, too, if she didn't agree to deliver a package into Chinatown for him."

Silent rage turned Emma's blood to ice as she mentally

counted to ten so as not to frighten away the already skittish teen. Mad Johnny, and the men like him, were a cancer that never failed to return if given the slightest invitation. Charlotte had been terrified of her former pimp, but somehow he'd gotten to her and that was what had likely gotten her killed. She smiled at Bella for her courage, hoping the action came off kindly instead of full of the malice she struggled to contain. "You've done a good thing in sharing this information with me, Bella. Thank you. Now, I want you to stop worrying. I will take care of this and share the information with Agent McIntyre so you don't have to." A look of gratitude flashed her way and Emma gestured toward the door. "Off to bed. It's late and you have a meeting with your counselor tomorrow. I know how you *love* those sessions and look forward to them."

It was said in a teasing manner as Bella hated talking with the "shrink" as she called the woman. But the therapy was working—if only in fits and starts—and Emma continued to insist that she attend the sessions. Besides, the fact that Emma required Bella to attend counseling created a favorable attitude in the courts, allowing Bella to remain in the house despite the unusual circumstances.

"I ain't tired and this ain't late. I've stayed up for days at a time without no one to tell me to…" Bella's grumble trailed as she closed the door behind her but Emma didn't mind. Somehow the surly teen had become special to her though she knew it was a mistake to allow herself to get so close. Still…it was hard to keep her distance when Bella needed someone in her life who liked her for who she was, not for her body or what they could get from her.

But as soon as Bella had gone, Emma growled a nasty expletive aimed at Mad Johnny and grabbed her cell phone. Fishing in her purse, she found Agent McIntyre's business card. The late hour meant nothing in her single-minded purpose. Without hesitation she dialed the cell number he'd scribbled on the back, and when he picked up she barely kept her temper in check as she said, "I have information you might find useful in your investigation. It seems Mad Johnny may have been blackmailing Charlotte. The girls have told me you'll find him at Sixteenth Street and Mission on most days. You'll know him by the bright purple Mohawk he wears. Feel free to use excessive force if he doesn't cooperate," she added with a little more heat than she would usually show to a stranger. Then she added with more calm, "Happy hunting, Agent McIntyre."

Chapter 4

Adrenaline hummed through his veins as Dillon traversed Mission and immediately spied the man known as Mad Johnny. It was hard to miss his punk purple Mohawk as the sleaze lounged against a light pole, his indolent stare sharp and slack at the same time. He was all seemingly gangly arms and legs but Dillon recognized the malice that rolled off him like a cheap cologne. This was a dirtbag of the first order. A sweep of his person and Dillon had already surmised he was likely packing a gun in his back waistband, hidden beneath the grungy leather jacket, and a switchblade in his faded jeans pocket. Dillon smiled. This ought to be entertaining. He liked to jack around with guys like Mad Johnny because they *always* underestimated him. Kara said it was the accent. He'd joked that was their mistake. Even guys with accents can kick ass.

"Hullo," he started congenially, walking over to the punk with a grin. "Got a minute?" Dillon cocked his head and waited to see which route the man would go. Would he tell him to bugger off or size him up for a sale? He hoped it was the first option. Dillon was itching for a little action. And he wasn't disappointed.

"Piss off, cop. Ain't against the law to stand here doing nothing," he said, slewing his gaze away, dismissing Dillon with a sneer that said, *you can't do shit and I know it.*

Except—and here's where it got fun—Dillon wasn't a cop. And he didn't much like to play by the rules.

He tsked. "Now that's not nice, Mad Johnny. Do your friends call you Mad or just Johnny? Or even John? Nicknames can be such a pain in the ass. My nickname was… Oh, right, you don't care about that. How about this? Screw the niceties and let's get to the point. I have questions and you're going to answer them nice and tidy-like or else things are going to get a little…uncomfortable."

"Uncomfortable?" Mad Johnny repeated, his lip curling with open scorn. "What are you going to do, cop? If you ain't got a warrant, I ain't answering shit. You savvy? Go find a doughnut shop somewhere and leave me alone."

So much for niceties. With a quick strike and twist, Dillon had busted the man's nose and then put him in a headlock to whisper in his ear, "See, your first mistake was not knowing the difference between a cop and an FBI agent with a nasty disposition." He tightened his hold and Mad Johnny's eyes bulged as he struggled to get free. "Your second mistake? I hate doughnuts. Clog your arteries. They're a heart attack with frosting. Now enough with the pleasantries…let's chat."

He released the man and Mad Johnny spun away, glancing at the people who were giving them a wide berth but not making a move to help. He must've realized he was in a bad spot. He gingerly touched his nose and winced, then glared at Dillon. "You broke it, you fu—"

"Hey...watch your mouth," Dillon warned, yet his lips twitched with the urge to dare him to push it. Damn, he was in a mood today. Mad Johnny bit back the expletive with a mutinous glare and then sucked back a wad of bloody snot with a wince. "That's better. I knew you'd see it my way with a little encouragement. Now tell me about your association with Charlotte Tedrow."

Mad Johnny dialed back the glare as he weighed his possible answers. A moment later he must've figured it would do no harm to answer with a groan about his nose. "She's my girl."

"You mean *was* your girl, right?"

A shaky but no less cocky grin spread across his lips but he lifted one shoulder. "Yeah...was."

Dillon considered the scum before him and speculated whether he knew about Charlotte's death. His instinct told him he didn't know. There was one way to find out. "Did you kill her?" The startled look said it all. The punk wasn't a very good liar, and Dillon didn't figure he was putting on a show for his benefit. Damn. Why couldn't it be simple? This tosser probably didn't have the brains required to finish a Scrabble game much less orchestrate a complex killing spree. "When was the last time you saw her?" he asked.

"Are you messing with me?" Mad Johnny demanded, but there was uncertainty in his bloodshot eyes. "I just saw her—"

"A few days ago when you forced her to deliver a package to Chinatown?" Dillon affected a bored expression but he watched the pimp with shark eyes. "Yeah, I know about that. What was in the package?"

"Aren't you supposed to take me down to the station or something if you're going to be interrogating me like this?"

Dillon waved his question away. "We're just talking, right?

But no worries. I'll have a uniform pick you up later when I find out what was in that package. Heroin? Meth? Pot? Did I hit the jackpot? So damn unoriginal. Not that I'd expect more from a grammar school reject like yourself but one can hope for a little variation on the usual theme."

Uncertainty crossed Mad Johnny's features as he tried to think of something equally insulting to counter with but his swelling nose tempered his mean streak as he finally spat, "Yeah? What do you know?" with a fair bit of nervousness.

"I know you're a small-time criminal with no brains and a taste for hitting women. You use as much as you sell which puts you in debt more often than you're flush and you're probably secretly homosexual considering your attitude toward women." He winked and the pimp's cheeks turned scarlet—whether from rage or embarrassment he wasn't sure—and Dillon shook his head. "As fun as it is playing around with your personal tragedy, I have work to do solving a murder and all that, but do yourself a favor and don't leave town. I suspect we're going to become well acquainted in the next few days."

"I didn't kill her," Mad Johnny blurted out, wiping at the watery red dribble coming from his nose. "You can't pin that on me. That bitch was always getting herself into trouble. If she's dead I didn't have nothing to do with it."

"Ironically, in spite of the fact that you're most likely a habitual liar, a thief and a drug addict, I believe you. Still… don't go anywhere."

"I ain't got nothing to hide," Mad Johnny shot back, but his eyes darted for an escape route, which gave him away. He was going to bolt, the little coward.

"If I have to find you…a broken nose will be the least of your worries, mate," Dillon warned, giving him another smile with the promise in his tone. "I'm a bit of a loose cannon, if you know what I mean. Rules? Eh. Like you…I find my way *around* them."

Mad Johnny sputtered but his pasty expression turned to gray dough and Dillon nearly laughed out loud. That felt good. His stomach growled, reminding him that he hadn't eaten breakfast. "I wonder if that bagel place is still around?" he mused, checking out the neighborhood, the pimp dismissed for now. Then he headed off in the direction his stomach required.

Emma was at her desk when Chick came in with the mail, a quizzical expression on her face. "This came in but there's no postage," she said, handing Emma the large, white envelope. Just as Emma reached for her letter opener, Chick stilled her hand, saying, "Maybe you should give it to the cops. What if it's anthrax or something?"

"Anthrax?" Emma repeated with a patient smile. "How would anyone we know get a hold of anthrax? It's not like you can buy it at the store. The stamp probably fell off in transit or something."

"Wait," Chick said, her eyes worried. "Why don't you call that FBI agent before you open it. I got a bad feeling."

"Chick…really?" Emma stopped and stared at her friend, prepared to tease her a little for being paranoid, but there was something about the true distress in Chick's eyes that gave her pause. Maybe Chick was right. "I suppose it wouldn't hurt to be safe rather than sorry," she conceded, setting the envelope aside. The relief on Chick's face was worth it, considering the emotional strain they were all suffering since Charlotte's death. "Anything else?" she asked, returning to the other mail.

"Yeah…Ursula was out last night. A john roughed her up." At that Emma bolted from her chair but Chick stayed her. "She's in her room and she doesn't want you to know. She's afraid you're going to kick her out."

"Why would she think that?" Emma asked, distressed. "Unless she broke the house rules. Did she?"

"No. She submitted a urine sample and I tested it. Came back clean."

Relief swept through her. As much as she stood by her rules, it killed her each time she had to send a girl packing for breaking them. And she'd come to care for Ursula…just like the rest. Mercy, she thought, her hand going to her forehead to massage away the tension. And it was still early in the day. "Does she need to go to the hospital?" she asked.

"I don't think so. Black eye, some pretty bad bruising but no broken bones."

Something to be grateful for, Emma thought with a grimace. Their hospital fund was dangerously low, as were all their line items in the budget, but that's how it was every year around this time before the annual winter ball fundraiser. Which reminded her, she realized with an unhappy private sigh…time to visit her parents.

"Keep an eye on her. Make sure she's comfortable and reassure her that she's not going to be kicked out, but I will need to see her sometime today to talk with her."

Chick nodded and then gestured at the envelope. "Let me know how that goes. If it's anthrax, you owe me a beer for saving your life," she joked.

Emma chuckled. "If it's anthrax, I'll buy you dinner."

"I'll take that bet," Chick said, but then gestured toward the foyer. "We have a visitor. Father Andre came by to talk with the girls."

Emma sighed. "Let me guess, Cari called him?" Chick nodded in answer and Emma pinched the bridge of her nose to stave off the headache that was bound to come after a visit from the friendly priest. Cari, known affectionately as Bambi because she had doe-brown eyes and looked as innocent as they came even though she was eight months pregnant, had found a kinship with the Catholic priest and had since started inviting the man to the house for spiritual guidance. While most of the girls tolerated his visits, Evie turned into a screaming shrew every time he came around. Emma rose and forced a smile. "I suppose I ought to say hello to our guest while you try and encourage Evie to stay in her room. I don't think I can handle that today."

"You got it," Chick said, leaving to head Evie off at the stairs while Emma went in search of Father Andre.

She found him sitting with Cari and Olivia, a Bible clasped between his palms, as he finished a prayer. He caught sight of Emma and rose, concern in his expression. "Ms. Vale, I came as soon as I heard…such terrible business. How are you holding up under the strain?"

"We're all holding up just fine, Father Andre," she answered, wishing she knew why she didn't particularly like the man. She forced a smile. "Thank you for coming to comfort Cari and Olivia."

"I'm here for you, as well," he reminded her with a kindly smile. "'If you are tired from carrying heavy burdens, come to me and I will give you rest. Take the yoke I give you. Put it on your shoulders and learn from me. I am gentle and humble and you will find rest. This yoke is easy to bear, and you will find rest because this burden is light.' Matthew 11:28–30."

She hated when he quoted Scripture at her. She'd never been particularly pious, though she didn't begrudge anyone the right to practice their faith, but when Father Andre whipped out his Scripture she never knew how to react. So she simply smiled and said nothing in return. Chick appeared at the top of the stairs and gave Emma a subtle nod indicating she'd handled Evie, for which Emma was tremendously grateful.

"Have the police discovered any leads as to who might have committed these heinous acts against God's wayward flock?"

Emma returned to Father Andre. "Well, the police are no longer investigating. The case has been handed over to the FBI and I don't know what they've discovered thus far."

"Let us pray that the Lord delivers swift and terrible justice to the wicked who have perpetrated these crimes," he said solemnly and Emma nodded in agreement. He gazed at her expectantly as he said, "Ms. Vale would you like to join us in our prayer circle today?"

She might've heard Chick smother a laugh but when she turned to glare at the woman, she was gone. Emma offered Father Andre an apologetic smile as she declined. "Too much to do, but I appreciate the offer. Please, stay as long as you like," she said, eager to leave but Cari stopped her.

"Father Andre offered to set up a Bible study if that's all right with you," she said, her brown eyes pleading, as she clasped her hands beneath the bulge of her rounded belly.

Emma withheld a sigh. She appreciated that Cari had found God with Father Andre's assistance and that Olivia—though she struggled with her vices—enjoyed the Catholic priest's visits, but she knew she'd have a riot on her hands with the other boarders if she allowed a Bible study in the house. "I'm sorry, Cari. You know I can't do that," she said, noting the thin line of disapproval forming on Father Andre's mouth. "Father Andre is always welcome to visit but I can't sanction a Bible study. You know not everyone is comfortable with organized religion and I won't willingly cause dissension in the house." She offered an apologetic look Father Andre's way but added, "Of course, Cari you are free to come and go as you please and if you would like to go to Bible study, then by all means, do."

Cari nodded, shooting an uncertain glance at Father

Andre as if she feared his reaction, and Emma took quiet note. Perhaps there was a reason she didn't quite care for the older gentleman that went beyond the clammy feel of his hands when he shook hers. She resolved to talk with Chick about her concerns. "Well, I just thought it would be nice to offer...." Cari's voice trailed off with a small shrug.

Emma smiled just as a knock at the front door sounded and she hastened to answer it. "That's very sweet of you, Cari. Now, if you'll excuse me..."

She knew it was Agent McIntyre on the other side of that door and the knowledge caused her heart rate to flutter in an odd show of nerves. *Oh, honestly!* She chastised herself before taking a deep breath and opening the door with the same sort of smile she'd offer a perfect stranger. This wasn't a social visit and she'd do well to remember that simple fact so as not to make a total fool of herself. She ushered him inside with a light chagrined laugh. "Thank you for coming, Agent McIntyre. I feel a bit silly but Chick insisted that I call...just in case..." She lifted her shoulders, not quite able to finish. Saying it out loud did in fact make her feel as if they'd overreacted, but on the off chance that someone truly meant them harm, she couldn't overlook it.

She met the agent's gaze and heat rose in her cheeks. Today, he seemed far more attractive than he had yesterday. How was that possible? There was something about him that made her think of things that she had no business entertaining, particularly under the circumstances. Yet, her stubborn mind refused to stop throwing her imagination into overdrive, wondering what she'd find under that jacket and shirt. She suspected her fingers might slide across a smooth, firm chest with very little hair to play with under her fingertips....

She hitched a short breath and her cheeks burned brighter as Agent McIntyre's eyebrows climbed slowly in response.

"Are you all right?" he asked.

"Yes. Of course." She forced a bright smile but her quivering insides told a different story. It was the extreme stress she was under, she rationalized. Easy enough to understand and even forgive. Feeling somewhat mollified, she gestured toward her office, eager to put an end to whatever was happening and return to the business at hand. "This way, please. The letter is in my office."

Dillon sensed there was something going on with Emma, but the sight of her at the door had sucked the air from his lungs in the most disconcerting way. Her long blond hair was swept in a neat ponytail away from her heart-shaped face, revealing high cheekbones that hinted at Nordic ancestry. She wore no-nonsense black slacks, yet the crisp, white shirt paired with a brilliant necklace strung from looping stones of turquoise sent *boring* galloping down the road to be replaced with *sexy* and *hot*.

She was thanking him and walking toward her office when he was finally able to tear his gaze away from her and shake himself back to normal. "I'm sure it's nothing," she said, more apology in her tone. "But everyone is on edge lately because of recent events and…well, it seemed prudent to make you aware."

"You made the right decision," he said, pulling a pair of gloves from his pocket and snapping them on as he approached the desk. He lifted the envelope carefully and using the sharp pewter letter opener, he slid it open and peered inside. "I think it's safe to assume there's no anthrax in here," he said, smiling, but there was something that put his nerves on edge. He was careful not to touch the envelope more than necessary. He pulled the letter free and gingerly set it aside. After determining there was nothing else in the envelope, he opened the letter.

"I think we need to get this to the lab," he said, his voice tight.

"What's wrong?" Emma asked.

He stared at the innocuous sheet of white paper, folded with three precise folds so that each crease matched perfectly and the familiar trickle of dread played a tune on his spinal cord.

Three words. Printed neatly. No signature.

Practice Makes Perfect.

The killer had just made contact with Emma Vale…and Dillon didn't like that one bit.

Chapter 5

Emma's mouth dropped open on a gasp and she took a faltering step backward as if whoever penned the cryptic note was going to spring from the page. "What does it mean?" she asked, though she had a pretty good idea. She just wanted Dillon to tell her she was wrong.

He didn't.

"Someone is trying to get your attention," he said grimly, tucking the letter back into the envelope before grabbing his phone from his pants pocket. He dialed before she could ask another question that she didn't want to know the answer to. "Yeah, I need an evidence kit and a team. I think the killer has made personal contact with Ms. Vale. I don't know…I'll find out. In the meantime, I need forensics. There might be some trace DNA left behind."

DNA, evidence…it was all too surreal to even digest properly. Why would someone send her something like this? Was it possible that someone was laughing at her expense?

Setting her nerves on edge simply for the entertainment value? But who would do such a thing? She couldn't imagine. Nor could she imagine why whoever had ended Charlotte's life was now fixating on her. Perhaps this was all a misunderstanding...

"You okay? You look a little pale," Dillon observed, his brows coming together as he pocketed his phone. She jerked a short nod but couldn't actually get the words to come out. He seemed to understand and took control. "Come sit a minute while you get over the shock. It's going to be all right," he promised as he guided her into a soft, high-backed chair farthest from the window. "We have the best team right here in San Francisco. If there's even a hint of DNA left behind, they'll find it. Now, tell me who brought you the mail this morning?"

"Chick. She always gets the mail for me," she answered, distressed. "She's the one who noticed that it didn't have any postage and cautioned me against opening it without you here."

"Smart woman," he said. "Where is she now?"

Emma swallowed a sour lump of something, likely fear, and after a glance at her watch, answered, "At the school, picking up Bella. She has a counseling appointment."

"I'll send a uniform to make sure that Chick is okay," he said, and Emma's eyes widened in alarm. He calmed her fears quickly. "Just as a precaution. We don't know what we're dealing with at this point, so we're going to act as if it's the worst-case scenario."

Emma nodded and gave him the addresses of both the school and the counselor's office. "Maybe this is just someone's idea of a really bad joke," she offered weakly. Lord, she hated how scared she sounded but even if her voice hadn't betrayed her, the tremor in her hands surely would have. She shook them out and blew a short breath, demanding some kind of inner strength show itself before she collapsed in an embarrassing fit of tears. "I have to warn the girls," she said, grasping onto something she knew. The safety of her boarders was her biggest concern. "They need to know what's going on."

"They will, but let's wait until we get some tests run on the letter first."

"Why?"

"Because we don't know anything about the sender. It could be someone in your own house."

She balked. "That's absurd."

"I appreciate your loyalty but until we rule everyone in this house out as a suspect, I'm going to have to ask that you refrain from sharing any information we might find." At her gathering frown, he added with sincerity, "I want to rule out the boarders as quickly as you. I'll make it my top priority."

"In other words, 'you don't have a choice but to follow my instructions,'" she said, chafing at his dictate. She wasn't accustomed to following someone else's lead, particularly when it came to her girls. "I understand you're following protocol or something of that nature but I know my boarders and there isn't one person in this house who'd do such a careless, cruel thing to me."

His jaw tensed. "You want to believe that everyone in this house is innocent—and so do I—but I'm not that naive. Sometimes the person we least suspect is the one plotting to put the knife in our back."

"Perhaps in your world, Agent McIntyre, but not here. We have a special relationship that is not only built on trust but sustained by it."

"Yeah, well, I'm not willing to take the chance so we'll do things my way because it's my investigation."

Her temper spiked but she quelled the fire before it got

the best of her. She believed he was off base suspecting any of her boarders, but until he figured that out on his own it would be a waste of breath on her part so she let it go, for the moment. "Fine," she conceded, but added a concession of her own. "I want to be there when you speak to them, particularly Bella. I won't compromise on this."

"I understand and that's agreeable. Gather them up. While the forensics team is collecting evidence, dusting for prints and whatnot, you and I will talk with the women together. I'll know whether or not they're lying."

"Is that so?"

"Yes."

"And how is that?"

"I'm trained as an interrogator. Facial cues, body language, voice inflections—combined they speak louder than words."

"Are you ever wrong?" she asked.

"Rarely."

A human lie detector. Emma suppressed a delicate shiver at the thought. She wasn't sure whether she found that arousing or terrifying. Perhaps a bit of both. She rose from the chair, thankful her knees had stopped quaking, and lifted her chin to say coolly, "Good to know, Agent McIntyre. I believe your team has arrived. Shall we meet them in the foyer?"

Dillon followed Emma into the foyer where the team was assembled. He didn't know this forensic team but he didn't need to know them on a first-name basis to know that they'd do their job well. All he had to do was point them in the right direction and they'd do the rest. And that's exactly what he did. His thoughts moved to Emma, wondering how she was faring under the strain.

He understood her feelings on the matter even if she

didn't voice them. He felt the same way. A part of him had been hoping that they weren't dealing with a true sociopath but rather an unimaginative nutjob who got his jollies by whacking a few prostitutes. People like that were sloppy. They were so wrapped up in the heat of their crimes that they always made mistakes. But the ones who were smart and devious were the ones Dillon wanted to avoid. The last one…had nearly cost him his own life along with Tana's. As much as he put on a good face, his veneer had cracked and he could only hide the stress fractures for so long.

"You okay?"

He turned at the concern in Emma's soft query, and the fact that she was inquiring after him instead of the other way around made him want to sink into his shoes. "Right as rain," he lied with a short smile. "Let's go talk to your boarders while details might be fresh in their minds."

She nodded but she watched him with that intense stare of hers that felt as if she were probing his mind. He waited for a half second to see if she'd voice her opinion or state her observations to the contrary but she did neither and he was grateful.

There were five women waiting for them in the kitchen, including Chick and Bella who had just arrived with an officer in tow, all wearing expressions of dread and confusion. "Is this everyone?" he asked before he began, but Emma's compressed lips told him not everyone was accounted for. "Who's missing?"

"Ursula," she answered, leaning over to Chick, who whispered something in her ear. She cleared her throat and said, "She's not feeling well. I'll talk to her personally when we're finished here."

"Unless she's incapacitated, I'd really like to have her down here. This won't take but a minute or two of her time."

Emma stiffened and he sensed he was poking at a mama bear. "If you're asking me to drag an ill young woman down here for your convenience then I'm sorry to disappoint you. It's not going to happen."

He weighed his options, relenting when he realized he had very little to gain by alienating Emma. "I apologize. Perhaps we could compromise. I can schedule some time to talk with Ursula in a day or two when she's feeling better."

It was the best he could do. He had to interview all the boarders. He hoped Emma realized this and conceded to his offer of compromise.

She glanced at Chick and he caught a minute change in her expression that said she was giving her grudging okay. The fact that Emma relied so heavily on Chick's opinion told him that the two were close. He knew very little of Chick aside from the short conversation they'd shared in the garden and it would be tough to get her to open up, but he hoped he'd gain some headway because if Chick locked him out, Emma would surely follow.

"I'm sure word travels fast so I'll get straight to the point. Ms. Vale received a letter today that may have been from the person responsible for Charlotte's death."

"Oh, God," breathed a pregnant blonde, her cherubic face paling with fear as her hands automatically rubbed her distended belly. Her gaze darted to Emma, whose distressed expression was probably not for herself but for the fear she read in their faces.

His intuition was dead-on as Emma turned to the young woman, who couldn't be older than eighteen, with all the reassurance she could muster in spite of the circumstances. "Don't worry, Cari. It could be a coincidence, a bad joke, a misunderstanding. We shouldn't jump to conclusions but we have to be cautious, as well." She shot him a look and he knew in an instant she wasn't going to withhold any details from her boarders. He mentally swore as she continued, "Agent McIntyre is having the letter sent to the FBI forensics lab to process it for any DNA that might've been left behind. Chick and I will give a DNA sample to rule out anything we've inadvertently left behind when we handled the envelope. This is a formality that we're happy to comply with. I want you to know we are doing our utmost to ensure everyone's safety. To that end, Agent McIntyre is going to need to speak with you all again. I appreciate your understanding and your cooperation. I know this is taxing for us all."

He supposed he could understand her loyalty to her girls, but it twisted his shorts in a knot that she'd deliberately disregarded his instruction to keep any and all information about the investigation under wraps. Unfortunately, he didn't have the time to take her to task on the subject. He caught her eye and she lifted her chin. She knew he was perturbed but didn't give a damn. He grudgingly admired her spirit even if he worried it would get her killed.

"So, let's say it is the killer…is he saying he's going to kill one of us? I mean, why would he put it in our mailbox?" demanded a black woman with short curled hair that frizzed at the ends, anger mixing with the panic in her voice. "I mean, it doesn't seem like a coincidence to me."

"I don't know, Olivia," Emma answered. "I wish I had the answers. I'm scared, too," she admitted, briefly meeting Dillon's gaze before returning to the group who were all looking to her. "Is there anyone who would like to volunteer to talk with Agent McIntyre first?"

Cari looked at her fellow boarders and when no one stepped forward, she hesitantly raised her hand. "I will," she said. "Whatever I can do to help. I don't want to be murdered in my bed. I have a baby to think about."

"The way this freak operates it won't be in your bed," quipped the black woman, earning a look from Emma.

"That's not necessary, Olivia, thank you," she lightly chided the woman into silence. She turned to Dillon. "You can use my office if you like."

"Thank you. Shall we?" He gestured, allowing room for the pregnant woman to pass and then followed her up to Emma's office. He wondered at the circumstances that had brought the teen to Iris House. It was likely a sad story. It appeared Emma plucked the ones she thought she could save from the streets. It only served to deepen the mystery that was Emma Vale—and increase his desire to know all that made her who she was and why.

Now he had a reason aside from personal interest to dig deeper.

The key to what was happening to those prostitutes might actually lie with Emma.

And that didn't sit well at all.

Chapter 6

He coveted.

An image of perfection, she never failed to brighten his day. The anticipation of their union slicked his hands and he had to rub them on his pant leg to dry the sweat.

Soon. He'd had so much fun with Charlotte. It was always such sweet sorrow when his dolls became broken. So pretty, so delicious.

But not fresh. No, those girls were dirty. Used and spoiled before they ever came into his possession. He watched and waited. Selecting his dolls with the utmost care. Everything had to be perfect. He was not an impatient man. He'd waited so long for Emma. One glance from her blue eyes and he'd been lost. And he knew. She was the one he'd been waiting for.

Even as he sat in the park, surrounded by people enjoying the view and the crisp yet clear San Francisco day, his enjoyment came not from the beautiful surroundings, but from his unobstructed line of sight.

A team of agents swarmed the front of Iris House, dusting for prints. His lip curled in disdain. As if he'd leave behind such easy evidence. He wished he'd been able to see her expression when she read his note. Had her pupils dilated with fear? Had she stared uncomprehending at the letter, wondering what it meant only to drop it in horror as the meaning became clear? She didn't know the honor he would bestow upon her. She would be the queen of his dolls. The only one worthy.

But first…he had work to do so that *he* was the worthy one.

It was late afternoon and Dillon wasn't finished interviewing her girls. Emma was on edge. Chick put a large Chai tea in her hand and she accepted it gratefully.

"How'd you know I desperately needed this?" she asked, taking a sip and closing her eyes briefly to savor the moment.

"It's been a rough day," Chick said, smiling as she sipped her own beverage that Emma knew would likely be some kind of premium roast so strong it could put hair on your chest. "And I needed one, so I figured, what the hell. A splurge on coffeehouse drinks seemed in order."

Emma wearily lifted her cup. "So true."

They drank in silence until Chick caught Emma glancing for the third time in as many minutes toward her office, where Dillon was interviewing the girls.

"Who's he with now?"

"Bella."

"I thought you were going to be sitting in on that meeting."

"I was. At the last minute, she said she wanted to do it alone."

Chick chuckled. "Did you frisk her for sharp objects first?"

Emma laughed at that. "I considered it but she's been pretty subdued today. I'm guessing therapy went well?"

"Well, she didn't come out spitting mad like she usually does. Maybe she hit a breakthrough. Or maybe she's contemplating all of our deaths while we sleep. You never know with that kid."

Emma's laughter died away at the sobering thought. Bella was so damaged. So broken. Sometimes she looked into those gorgeous eyes and saw desolation staring back at her. It only served to strengthen her need to help put her pieces back together. Hope drove Emma with a master's whip, demanding everything from her, and she gladly gave it—most days. But for a selfish moment, she wished for something that was far less absorbing than the endless struggle to save girls from the streets, and themselves. She exhaled softly but kept her thoughts private where they belonged. Without her, Iris House would crumble and what then? Iris House had become more than her passion and redemption…it'd become her life. She couldn't let it fail for any reason—personal or otherwise. She shuddered at the thought.

"You know, if she keeps up the violent outbursts at school, they're going to pull her from your care," Chick said, interrupting her thoughts, for which Emma was glad.

"They can try," Emma said, the light tone betraying the thread of steel. She was willing to fight tooth and nail to keep Bella. Everyone in that girl's life had given up on her; she wasn't going to be another in a long line.

Chick sighed, the sound pulling at Emma. She knew Chick worried that she was being reckless because of her feelings for Bella. She couldn't deny it. "She's not Elyse," Chick said quietly.

A pain so raw and angry slapped Emma and it took a moment before she could speak without her voice betraying her. Leave it to Chick to pull no punches. She had to remind herself at times that she appreciated that facet of the woman's personality. "I know that."

Chick held her stare. "Do you?"

"Yes, Chick," she answered but she didn't have the guts to hold her best friend's gaze. Chick might be younger than her by a few years but she saw too much. She knew. The sound of her office door opening gave her a reprieve from where the conversation was going. She jumped to her feet and rushed into the hallway to catch Bella's expression. The teen looked deceptively fine. "Everything all right?" she asked, striving for a normal tone but her nerves were strung taut.

"He wants to see you," Bella said. "And yes, I'm fine. Stop treating me like I'm some kind of basket case." She looked to Chick. "Is there any food? I'm starved."

Emma pursed her lips. Perhaps Bella had a point. She had been hovering. She'd hate that, too. She gestured to the kitchen, saying, "You can heat up the leftover spaghetti Cari made last night during one of her late-night cravings. She made enough to feed an army."

She opened the door to her office and found Dillon standing by the wide window that graced her south wall. His profile, sleek and sinewy without looking feminine, cut an impressive silhouette that was hard to overlook. Her thoughts raced without her permission to all sorts of things she imagined he was good at without the encumbrances of clothing. Perhaps it was because he was a foreigner. She'd always been a little weak for the ones with an accent. There was also the mystery. How did an Englishman come to join the FBI? Of course, those were personal questions and none of her business but the curiosity remained.

"How'd the interviews go?" she asked, almost loath to pull him away from his thoughts. Was he thinking of someone special? She suspected it was hard to keep a relationship going with the long hours and dangerous cases he worked but it wasn't impossible. Especially given that he was devastatingly handsome. Devastating? *Oh, truly, Emma. You're sinking fast into melodramatic territory.* He was passing attractive. Perhaps a little too slim for her tastes. No, that wasn't true at all. She found men who were covered with lumps of muscle to be off-putting but he surely filled out his clothes nicely. She cut sharply away to take a seat behind her desk. "I assume none of the girls gave you any trouble," she said, trying to keep the worry or distraction from her voice. Evie and Bella were her prime suspects in the trouble department. Either one could deliberately become difficult with the switch in the wind.

Instead of answering, he startled her with a statement. "You have interesting criteria for your boarders at Iris House. Has it always been this way?"

"Whatever do you mean?" she asked, folding her hands neatly in front of her, if only to keep the trembling hidden. He affected her in the worst way. Plain and simple, she was wildly attracted to him. She was an adult; she could admit it. But where did that put her? In a terrible predicament. It could go nowhere and she wasn't in a habit of being casual so she had no choice but to bottle that annoying little jitterbug in her stomach and move on as if it had never been acknowledged.

"A pregnant woman, a drug addict—"

"A recovering drug addict," she corrected automatically.

He lifted a brow at the correction and continued.

"*Recovering* drug addict, a surly teen with a record, a working prostitute and an ex-con…not your typical sorority house."

"We pride ourselves on that," she said, taking careful note that although he hadn't talked to Ursula he had found out that she was still hitting the streets. It made her wonder what else he had gathered from the girls. "They all have a past…but that doesn't mean they can't have a future."

"Is that the Iris House motto?" he asked.

She couldn't tell if he was mocking her but it didn't feel much like a compliment. She regarded him coolly. "Did you find what you were looking for?"

He seemed to catch that he'd offended her. Something flickered across his gaze—regret, curiosity—she wasn't sure, but he didn't give her the chance to find out. Pushing his hand through his hair, he shook his head with a weary sigh. "No."

"So my girls are clear?" Relief was immediate as he answered with a nod.

"All except Ursula," he added. He moved away from the window but leaned against the wall. He was the most puzzling man she'd ever come across. She didn't have a habit of working with FBI agents but Dillon McIntyre wasn't what she would've imagined if she were drawing a picture. He managed to make *slouching* look sexy. She straightened her own spine. He gazed at her, tucking his hands in his trouser pockets. "Any particular reason why you got all snarly earlier? I sense a story."

She shouldn't tell him. It was Ursula's business but he was bound to find out eventually and she didn't want to make it seem as if she'd been hiding anything. She drew a short breath before answering. "Ordinarily, I wouldn't divulge such personal information but due to the extraordinary circumstances I feel it may be pertinent to share. Ursula has remained in her room because she is recuperating from an unfortunate incident with a…client." She met his inquiring gaze evenly, without reservation. "She was beaten by a john. Severely."

If she expected recriminations she didn't get any, which elevated Dillon a fraction in her estimation. She was even willing to give him extra points for the dark frown of concern pulling his brows as he asked, "She okay?"

Emma drew away, leaning back in her chair, the day wearing on her reserves. "She'll live. Chick said she's bruised pretty badly but nothing is broken."

"I'm surprised you didn't take her to the hospital."

"I would've. Ursula refused medical treatment. I respected her wishes."

"She should've made a police report for assault," he said, but they both knew why she didn't. Prostitutes who got banged up during the commission of a crime weren't usually given the red carpet treatment. Emma had witnessed the prejudice firsthand with her sister. Her mouth tightened as the memory bloomed and it took great will to keep her comments on the subject from spilling out. If he noted her reaction he didn't push. He seemed to realize she was skirting something personal and even if his eyes lighted with interest in the mystery he simply returned to the business at hand. "Since Ursula is unavailable tonight for questioning, that leaves my evening open for you."

A jolt of something hot and unfamiliar sparked along her nerve endings but she managed a sensible agreement. He needed to interview everyone in the house; that included her. There was nothing above and beyond protocol that prompted his statement, and if his gaze seemed to linger it was only because he was trained to watch for subtlety, not because he was checking her out. What a thought. She suppressed a melancholy sigh that came from out of nowhere.

"Of course," she said, gathering her hands in her lap, prepared to answer whatever question he might pose. "I expected as much. What would you like to know?"

He zeroed in on her gaze, pinning her with that dark and unwavering stare and she could've sworn her heart stuttered a beat. It was hard to look away but she schooled her expression into one of neutrality even if every nerve snapped and sizzled at the raw heat that emanated from those eyes.

"Are you dating anyone?"

So much for finesse. So much for protocol. But Dillon needed to know. He had his reasons. Ones that were grounded in logic. But he couldn't lie. He had reasons that were purely selfish, too.

The pink tip of her tongue snaked out to touch her top lip, as if without thought and his body hardened. *Get a hold of yourself, man. Your cheese has done slid off your cracker.*

"Uh..." She faltered at the personal question he'd lobbed at her with all the grace of an elephant but she shook her head in answer. "No. I don't have time for much of a personal life. Iris House is a large commitment that leaves little room for...much else. Why?"

"Is there anyone—rebuffed suitors, angry ex-boyfriends—who might have a score to settle with you?" he asked. In theory, a less-secure man might find her rejection too much to handle. He needed to rule out former flames as suspects. "Anyone who might have suffered a broken heart?"

"At my hands?" Her mouth twisted in a small but wry smile. "No. Like I said, I haven't had much opportunity to break hearts or enjoy company."

He tucked that away, absurdly relieved. But he also found it telling. "Why would someone—pardon my saying—who is as attractive, intelligent and accomplished as you remain single?"

"Agent McIntyre, I was raised in an age where a woman doesn't need a man to feel complete," she answered with a smile. She was playing with him but he saw the loneliness that she tried to hide, burying it under work, obligation and responsibility. She continued with a shrug. "Besides, it isn't as if I've avoided dating. I just value my time and have rarely found anyone worth sacrificing it for." In theory it sounded plausible but he sensed a ghost lingering in the room, something that constantly pushed her to relegate her needs to the farthest corner and he wanted to know why.

"But you would if you found the right person?"

A small, tremulous smile followed. "Are you asking me out, Agent McIntyre?"

He straightened. "No. Just trying to figure a few things out."

"Let me make it simple for you," she said, rising. "Iris House means everything to me. I would never jeopardize the success and stability of the house for the sake of personal involvement. I'm a busy woman, as you can imagine. I hardly miss the complications inherent in a relationship."

That was a bold-faced lie. At least part of it was.

And he wanted to know what was behind door number two. He just had to figure out how to get the key.

Chapter 7

Emma took a moment to compose herself before she pushed the doorbell on her parents' palatial home, stuffing down the trepidation that usually followed a visit to Veronica and Nigel Vale.

It wasn't always so difficult to go home but after Elyse died—she swallowed the familiar lump when thoughts of her sister arose—and the opening of Iris House, the visits became more like tense negotiations rather than family get-togethers. And frankly, as her parents aged, they became less interested in tact than they were in their single-minded desire for her to shut down Iris House and take her place in society, as if they were living in the Victorian age and Emma was shaming them for her career choice.

She had no taste for pointless dinners and parties. Perhaps at one time she'd been seduced by the lavish social events, but after Elyse died Emma had realized how shallow and meaningless it all was. She also recognized that to keep

Iris House open she had to continue to circulate in the same nauseating circles as she had before, only now she was more interested in their generous donations.

The door opened and she smiled a greeting to Phillipe, their butler since she was a child, and allowed him to take her coat.

"So good to see you, Miss Vale. Your parents are enjoying a cocktail in the drawing room with Mr. West," Phillipe said, his voice strong in spite of the full head of silver and the fact that he suffered terrible arthritis in his hands. She paused for a moment. "Isaac is here? I thought he was still out of town," she mused.

"Apparently, his business concluded early and he heard of your troubles and wanted to show his support."

"How sweet of him," she said, smiling.

"Yes," Phillipe agreed amiably, adding, "Perhaps he will provide a welcome buffer should things become… uncomfortable with your parents."

"Yes, perhaps," she said smothering a giggle, resisting the urge to hug the older gentleman. With her parents milling about she didn't dare embarrass Phillipe with such a display. But Phillipe was as much a part of her childhood as was Maura, the family cook, and she refused to ignore that fact simply because they were in a different tax bracket. "How are you, Phillipe?" she asked, taking note of the subtle stiffness in his gait. "Are you using that cream I sent for your joints? I found it in Chinatown. It's supposed to be wonderful for arthritis. And since I got it from a little old Chinese lady who swore by it, I figured it was worth a try."

He bent his head ever so slightly and a smile played on his lips. "It's very soothing, Miss Vale. If you'll allow me to take the cost out of my paycheck I'd be most obliged."

"I will not, which is why I won't tell you how much it cost because I know you'll try and slip me the money somehow. Besides, it was very little and I'm happy to do it." She savored the warm feeling in her chest for just a moment as she enjoyed being able to help in some way. Then with an inward sigh to bolster her nerves she asked, "So what's the mood in there?" Phillipe's brow furrowed as if troubled and that gave her pause. Usually, Phillipe didn't mind giving her a heads-up on the sly but now he clearly seemed bothered by something. She paused. "What's wrong?"

"This business with that maniac killing the ladies of the night has everyone worried about you, Miss Vale. Your parents have been glued to the television each night, waiting for news, hoping that whoever is perpetrating these horrific crimes has been caught." Phillipe placed a hand gently on her shoulder, and her eyes widened at the genuine concern she read in his dignified face. "They're terrified of losing you, too."

"Likely, they're more terrified of the bad press," she said in an uncharitable grumble that immediately shamed her, but the old arguments her parents resurrected about Iris House caused her to be defensive.

"I shouldn't talk out of turn but Mr. Vale pulled some considerable strings to ensure your safety regarding this nasty business."

She startled. "What do you mean?"

Phillipe shook his head. "I've said too much already. It's not my place, but I know I rested a little easier knowing the FBI had assigned their best to the case. Just remember your parents have already lost one daughter—they can't bear to lose another."

Elyse's ghost hovered between them, a painful memory for the entire household. As much as she was loved, her death had been both devastating and a relief for her parents. By the last days, Elyse had nearly ripped their family apart. Emma read the pain in Phillipe's eyes as the memory haunted him, as well. She buried the cold knot of fear pulsing beneath the surface of her emotions and deliberately forced a warm smile for his concern. It hurt her heart to see Phillipe so visibly shaken. She patted his soft, gnarled hand and reassured him as best as she could. "You've nothing to worry about, Phillipe," she said with good cheer, though she didn't quite like the fact that her father had been responsible for putting Dillon on the case. It made her feel babysat and that didn't sit well at all. Still, since she had no wish to trouble Phillipe with her feelings on the matter, she simply reassured him. "I am taking every precaution. Agent McIntyre is quite sharp and you'd like him, I think. He's very 007 with his British accent but there's an edge about him that says *I can disable you with my pinkie*." She refrained from continuing. There were many things about Dillon McIntyre that were noteworthy, but if she continued, Phillipe knew her well enough to see that she was soft on the man. And she didn't really want anyone to know that. Least of all her family. She had complications enough. She didn't need one more added to the heap.

Phillipe's frown didn't ease, but he remained silent, offering only the slightest nod to indicate he'd said his piece even if he didn't feel better about the situation.

She sighed and glanced in the direction of the drawing room. "Guess we should get this over with. The Vales are not the kind of people you leave waiting." She offered a subtle mischievous smile, which Phillipe couldn't help but return.

Lips twitching, he said, "This way, Miss Vale. It's always a pleasure."

Phillipe announced her at the door and then closed it behind him. Her parents, as well as their family friend Isaac West stopped their conversation and turned as she walked into the room.

Isaac, a wealthy gentleman who had come into their lives through her father's business associates, had been something of an uncle to Emma and Elyse, and she was, at the very least, happy to see him, if not her parents.

He greeted her with an effusive hug that caused her to laugh when it lingered. "Isaac, you act as if you haven't seen me in years," she joked when he finally let her go.

"Forgive me, but you get more beautiful each time I see you," Isaac said, his gaze warm and appreciative. She laughed away his compliment but he would not allow it. He shook his head. "No, it is no wonder your father cringes at the company you keep."

Faltering, Emma glanced at her parents, wondering when they'd managed to contaminate Isaac's views on her work when he'd always been so supportive, even going so far as to help find the building for Iris House when she first began. "Isaac, please tell me you haven't lost faith in the work I do," she teased but there was unease resting beneath the surface. She needn't have worried, though. A heartbeat later Isaac laughed and waved away her concern.

"Of course not. It's just this sordid business has everyone all tied in knots. You are a guardian angel for those women," he declared, ignoring her father's look of irritation at his effusive praise. "Nigel, deny it all you want…Emma is doing important work. Imagine how things might've been different if there'd been something like Iris House for Elyse?"

Veronica Vale stiffened at the mention of Emma's twin, the subject forever a sore one for her mother. She sniffed and took a quick sip of her wine. "Next subject," she demanded, her displeasure clear. "I will not have a pleasant evening ruined by bad memories."

Emma swallowed her immediate ire for Isaac's sake, but a moment of uncomfortable silence followed until Veronica cleared her throat and forced a smile like the good hostess she was trained to be. "Darling, it's so good to see you. What's new? Anything exciting going on? Isaac was just telling us that on his latest trip he rode an elephant."

Emma shot Isaac a look of incredulity that was not entirely directed at his mode of transportation while visiting Thailand. She chose her words carefully, not wanting to incite a full-blown fight when there was a guest in the house but not wanting to pretend that everything was fabulous for the sake of appearances. "Well, Mother, as you know, we've suffered a loss at Iris House," she began. "So we've been wrapped up in the investigation. An agent has been interviewing the girls—"

"Emmaline," her mother's sharp voice interrupted her, her mouth a firm slash of Estée Lauder red. "I don't want to talk about Iris House tonight. Surely, there's something else happening in your life worth talking about aside from *prostitutes* and *drug addicts*."

"Veronica, don't needle the girl," Nigel cut in, while Isaac looked pained to be in the same room with the Vales at the moment. Likely, he hadn't expected the evening to deteriorate the way it was. "You're always complaining that she doesn't visit enough as it is. Why are you trying to scare her off?"

"I just don't want to talk about that place," Veronica said in a low tone, rising to refill her wineglass. "The whole thing makes me sick to my stomach, especially now with that maniac running around."

"Emma, we've come to the conclusion that this sordid business—" he gestured at her with a wave of his hand that she knew to mean Iris House "—has to stop. It was a harmless hobby that was quite benevolent of you in the beginning, but there's real danger now with that man on the loose and I don't want you in the thick of it."

"Now, Nigel—" Isaac started but her father waved him off.

"No, Isaac, you've been out of the country for a while. You

don't know what kind of danger Emma has gotten herself wrapped up in. I'm sorry but things have gotten serious."

"Dad..." She spoke around the growing tightness in her chest and tried not to let her temper get the best of her. Her father was notorious for being a controlling bully but she was no longer a teenager under his thumb and refused to be cowed. "I appreciate your *concern,* but really, the media has sensationalized the case and I'm not in any danger. Besides," she couldn't help but add even when she'd told herself to let it go, "from what I hear you pushed all the right buttons to get the best on the case, so I should be *just fine.*"

"Emma, the prostitute that was killed," her mother started, her tone faltering on the word *prostitute* as if just allowing the word to fall from her lips was some kind of social faux pas, and shooting a glance at Nigel, who was wearing his customary hard-lipped scowl. "We know she was one of your boarders. Charlotte, yes?" Veronica took her silence as enough of an admission. "This is hitting too close to home. We can't allow you to continue putting yourself in harm's way with this pet project."

Pet project? "I beg to differ, Mother. Iris House is beyond a pet project or hobby. We're making a difference out there for the women who want to change their lives. I appreciate your concern but I have no intention of shutting down."

"Don't make us be the bad guys when we're just trying to keep you safe," her mother said, puzzling Emma. The decision was not theirs to make. They held no claim on Iris House, she'd made sure of that from the beginning, yet there was an uncomfortable buzz at the base of her skull that surely wasn't a good sign. "Your father and I think it would be best if you moved home for a while. Until things settle down and everything goes back to normal."

Move home? She was an adult, not a child and it irked her to know that in spite of her achievements her parents still perceived her as a girl who needed a short leash lest she hurt herself. "No." Her answer was immediate. Leave Iris House? Absolutely not. "That's not possible. I have responsibilities. You may not understand but I can't just walk away. It's ridiculous for you to even assume that I would consider it."

"Ridiculous?" Nigel repeated, his brow darkening. "What I find ridiculous is your incessant need to cling to a bunch of drug-addled whores, one of which was found cut to pieces, when it's clearly unsafe to do so."

Isaac jumped to her defense. "Nigel, my friend, you aren't being entirely fair. Emma's work is incredibly important. You should be proud of her."

"Thank you, Isaac, but don't waste your breath," she said, too angry to censor her words, fisting her hands as she directed her ire at her father. "Don't talk about my boarders with such disrespect. You know nothing about Iris House and with that attitude you never will." She gathered a deep breath, her body quaking with the rage that her father never failed to kindle with his elitist snobbery, and cooled her voice with great effort. She wasn't going to let him goad her into a shouting match. "If that's all this visit was about then we're finished here."

"Emma, please," her mother said, a plea in her voice as her gaze darted from Emma to her husband. "What your father is trying to say is that it's just too dangerous right now."

Emma thawed just a little at the raw fear in her mother's voice. Veronica was not putting on a show for her benefit. Wonder of all wonders, her mother's concern was genuine. Immediately shamed for her unkind thought, she said, "That's what I'm trying to tell you…I'm fine. I'm in no danger whatsoever. I'm just as safe here as I am at Iris House and I have too much to do before the Winter Ball to skip out now, even for a short time. Mother, surely you can understand the preparations that go into coordinating a major fundraising event."

"Of course," Veronica said. As the cochair or chair of a multitude of events throughout the city from her various committees and women's groups, this was something she was quite aware of and could sympathize with. "But, perhaps you could put someone else in charge of the Winter Ball this year. I've always thought you needed to delegate more anyway."

"You could be right but you know I won't," she said. "I'm too much like the woman who raised me. I need to be involved with every detail. You've always said that to ensure a job is done correctly, you must do it yourself. I take that advice to heart." *If nothing else,* she nearly muttered to herself. Emma had often wondered if the decision to adopt her and Elyse had been based on a need to accessorize with the latest fashion trend, which at the time happened to be babies.

Her father eyed her with the same steady stare that left board members of the family's pharmaceutical company quaking in their expensive Italian loafers and said tersely, "Don't bother lying, Emmaline. I know about the letter. Someone is fixating on you and I won't have my last remaining heir sliced to pieces at the hand of some maniac. End of story. You're coming home."

Chapter 8

By the time she returned to Iris House, it was dark, she was emotionally exhausted and she couldn't keep the tears from falling. She dashed the moisture from her cheeks in an angry gesture as she made her way to her floor, thankful that everyone was in their own rooms and not walking about the halls. She didn't need them to see her in this way.

She prided herself on being the consummate professional, the cool head in the midst of crisis, but right about now she was nowhere near calm nor cool and she couldn't trust her mouth. When was her father going to learn that she was not a child any longer and that he had no control over her life? Hadn't their struggles with Elyse taught him anything? Apparently not. He was still trying to run everyone's life with or without their consent. He hadn't even attempted to appear as if her feelings mattered on the subject. He'd just demanded that she leave Iris House and come home. If anything, his bullying had only worsened after Elyse's death. She stopped short of blaming him for what happened to her sister but she came skidding damn close to that thought. Elyse had had many problems but their father had compounded them with his high-handed attitude.

Emma had stormed out of her parents' house riding fast and hard on indignant anger but beneath that a frisson of alarm shivered through her at what her father might do to persuade her to shut down Iris House. He had powerful friends and a long arm. She'd do anything to keep Iris House running, but in the end, if he started contaminating her donation pool…he could sabotage her best efforts to keep it going.

Hands shaking, she closed the door behind her, still fuming about how things went down with her parents and fearful of what the consequences might be, so it took her a full second to realize the door had been unlocked. Heart leaping into her throat she nearly stumbled and fell on her rump when she saw Dillon lounging on her sofa as if he had every right to be there.

"Excuse me?" she managed to gasp, her hand going to her throat where her pulse beat against the soft skin as if trying to escape. His attire shouldn't have looked sexy—a rumpled burgundy dress shirt and a loosened tie generally looked sloppy to her—but at that moment she was shocked by how delectable he appeared even when she knew it was highly inappropriate. Maybe that was the allure. She had a healthy dose of *damn-the-consequences* running through her veins and she was barely holding on to a very slim thread of professionalism. "What are you doing here, Agent McIntyre?" *In my room. At this hour.*

He unfolded himself from the sofa with an apologetic expression though his gaze traveled her face and noted the wet cheeks. "Chick put me in here to wait for you. Said it was best since the girls were still a little wary of my company."

He paused, giving her a chance to offer an explanation for her tears, but when she just lifted her chin and remained silent he continued with only the subtlest of lifted brows. "I've taken it upon myself to ensure your safety. There's an agent outside the perimeter and I volunteered to be the agent on the inside."

"And why would you do that?" she asked. Her stomach muscles twisted at the silken slide of his voice. Nerves taut and raw from the bout with her parents, she couldn't stop from eyeing him with the hunger that simmered just below the surface of her carefully painted veneer of control. There was a recklessness that was altogether heady and frightening but she was too emotionally wrought to tamp it down. For once she wanted to do what felt good instead of what was expected and as her gaze traveled his tall, lean body, she knew with a tingle in her fingertips what would feel like heaven.

"Because I take my job very seriously," he answered softly.

"How lucky for me to have someone so diligent in charge of my safety." She was always looking out for everyone else, making sure the women in the house had what was needed to survive. Her own needs had taken a backseat and she'd been fine with the inevitable end of her social life, but right about now, those needs were superseding just about everything else, including common sense.

"Of course, if you're uncomfortable—" he started, mistaking her comment for one of censure. She almost smiled at his consideration but she knew it would come off looking slightly feral so she didn't. Instead, she took a step toward him, her heart hammering hard against her chest and increasing that whole breathless feeling that was making her light-headed, and before he could fathom what she had in mind, she launched herself at his mouth.

Indeed, her sudden action startled him and as he stumbled and the back of his legs caught against the sofa edge, he tucked her into his arms before he fell, dragging her down with him. He took the impact of their fall, hesitating only a fraction of an instant, his lips stilling as if weighing the consequences. But she wasn't interested in rational thinking at the moment and coaxed his tongue from his mouth.

Their tongues tangled, the glide and tease heating her blood and torching her internal body temperature until her clothes scratched and weighed heavily on her limbs. A small voice cautioned her to stop, to think about the outcome of such rash action but she ruthlessly stomped the life out of that voice and thrilled when Dillon's hand found the rounded curves of her rear and clamped down possessively.

"This is a terrible idea," he growled against her lips even as he pulled her closer, digging that hard length of his against the hottest spot in her body, causing her to groan and rub against him for that delicious friction. "There are rules—" his mouth broke away from her lips to travel the column of her neck "—against this sort of thing. Bad, so bad…we should stop…protocol…procedure…ethics."

If she was going to do this she'd rather not be distracted by talk of consequences. She nodded as if she agreed and then reached between them to grasp at his erection straining against the zipper of his trousers. She smiled when he jerked and moaned at the teasing contact. "You were saying, Agent McIntyre?"

"I was saying…" he murmured.

She pressed little kisses along his jawbone to his lips, inhaling the unique scent of his skin, impatient to get him out of his clothes and into her bed before she completely returned to her senses and realized what a mistake this was.

"Oh, bloody hell," he said, rising to meet her lips in a hard, openmouthed kiss that shot sparks of red-hot lust straight south, searing a path down her synapses until she completely lost any inkling of pulling back. She'd already vaulted over the line of propriety...there was no sense in stopping now. Besides, she'd never been one to do things halfway, so when they rolled to the floor, their fall cushioned by the plush carpet, she simply closed her eyes and told herself she'd deal with the aftermath...later.

Much later.

Dillon stared at the ceiling, his chest still rising and falling sharply from the workout he'd just given to—and received from—the woman who was lying beside him and wondered what had come over him that he was willing to sacrifice his bollocks for a wick dipping. Albeit a fantastic, mind-blowing wick dipping but...holy shite. He'd done screwed himself out of a career in grand style and yet...he hadn't jumped up, grabbed his clothes and split like he probably should've.

For that matter, she hadn't kicked him out yet, either.

"I don't do this," she said, breaking the silence.

"The random sex with a handsome stranger who's in charge of your protection from a possible serial killer?" When she nodded slowly, he shrugged. "That makes two of us."

She rolled to her side to face him. "I'm not joking," she said. Her nakedness seemed to be a nonissue, which in spite of his British roots he found quite refreshing. Either that or he just enjoyed the view.

"Neither am I," he returned with mild affront. "I'm not that kind of girl."

"You're joking again. Be serious, please."

"Now, where's the fun in that?" he retorted, but when she failed to smile he sighed and said, "All right. Serious faces now. What would you like to talk about? I'm all yours for the next…oh, eight hours. After that I'll have to check my calendar."

"Where are you from?" she asked, gazing at him with that steady stare that had nearly mesmerized him the first time they met over the unfortunate circumstance of a body identification.

"Hammersmith, London."

"London," she said, testing the word on her tongue. Then she looked at him quizzically. "How did a Londoner find himself in the FBI?"

"My parents split when I was a lad and my father moved to the States while my mum stayed in London. I had dual citizenship until I became of age and when it came time to choose, I became a U.S. citizen. From there, it was the same as anyone else who decides to join the Bureau."

"Do you ever visit your mother?"

"Every summer. She'd skin me alive if I didn't," he said with a smile. "Why?"

She shrugged. "Just curious. Are you close?"

He thought of his mum with her upper-class upbringing and all the silly things she considered important and grinned. "Yeah, she's a card. I find her endless attempts to find me a wife entertaining." He wondered at the odd questions given the way they'd spent the past two hours, tangled up in each other. He tossed one question her way. "What's with all the questions? And since you're feeling chatty, why were you crying earlier?"

She considered both questions a moment, and he thought she was going to blow him off. But she didn't. She answered with a small sigh. "I figured I should know at least a little about the man I just slept with. And the reason I was crying… that's not a very interesting story."

He lifted a brow. "I don't recall much sleeping. Though I am a bit wore out at the moment, and a nap does seem the thing but let me be the judge of what's interesting or not. Chances are I'll find the reason riveting."

"It's just family stuff. My father is an overbearing control freak with a limitless checking account. He and I had a disagreement and I let it get to me more than I should."

"See? You were wrong. Fascinating."

She chuckled. "Agent McIntyre—"

He interrupted her with a finger against her lips. "Now here's where I must insist that you call me Dillon. Agent McIntyre is so pre–sexual contact. We can't possibly go back to that time now that I've seen your naughty bits. It's just not possible."

"Not possible?" she repeated, a small smile playing at the corners of her mouth. "Sure it is. We'll just pretend that it didn't happen."

"Ah, but for that to work I'd have to be a good liar, and while I don't know about you, I'm a terrible liar."

"Well, you're lying right now, so I'd say you're pretty good at it because you seem quite earnest in your declaration that you can't lie."

He couldn't help himself and leaned forward, asking softly, "And what makes you think that?" His lips hovered near hers, a scant breath away.

"Because you work for the government," she answered before closing the distance and sealing her mouth to his.

Can't argue that, he thought, his body leaping to life, ready for round three…er…four with an eager surge of blood to his shaft. She straddled his hips, that warm, wet center causing him to strain for control as he tried to recall the many important reasons why he should put a stop to this reckless behavior. But when she sheathed him completely, her eyelids fluttering shut as a moan escaped her parted lips, rational thought fled. And he didn't really give a damn about good sense or the rules because, hell, beautiful women were meant for loving and rules were meant to be broken.

Chapter 9

Emma let the hot water sluice over her deliciously aching body, each twinge and lingering soreness a reminder of the hot interlude with the agent she'd left snoring lightly in her bed. After another tumble on the floor they'd guzzled some Gatorade and headed to the bedroom for more, as her knees had picked up some uncomfortable rug burns in their escapades and she'd been ready for the soft cushion of her pillowtop.

But even as she savored the memory of last night, the reality of what they'd done was harsh in the morning light. Two hands above her head against the shower wall, she closed her eyes and allowed the water to pour over her in the hopes of washing away her reckless behavior. She didn't hear the shower door open, but when she felt familiar yet strange hands reaching around and cupping her breasts, she swallowed a groan as he drew her close to his hard body and his erection pressed against her bottom. This was crazy, she ought to say to him. But the man was doing insanely wonderful things with his fingers and it was hard to actually form the words that would complete the sentence.

She was already slick and her knees wobbled.

"Careful now, showers are dangerous places," he said against her neck, the steam filling the room with sensual warmth. "It's a good thing I came in here…it seems you need a little help."

The water, his fingers, and her own greedy need eclipsed her good intention of informing him that last night was a onetime deal. "Ohhh, no fair," she panted against the tightening of her muscles as an orgasm crested before she realized it was so close and sent her sagging against Dillon's smooth chest. It took her a moment to catch her breath, but once she did, she pulled away and with a silent request for strength, turned and met his gaze.

His erection bobbed as he grinned a good-morning. He was devilishly handsome, she noted almost clinically. Not her usual type for certain but there was an undeniable magnetism to his lazy, cocky smile that drew her to him with startling speed. As she formulated a speech in her head, her gaze was drawn to the thick, engorged shaft that she'd become intimately familiar with in a very short amount of time and her resolve weakened. Her hand curled around it before she realized her intent and using a bit of soap for lubrication, she repaid the favor.

Shower finished, Dillon and Emma dressed apart. He sensed her pulling away even as she'd pumped his shaft to completion, and he couldn't blame her. He wasn't sure he knew what the hell had come over him, but while he should've been relieved that she was ready to pull the plug, he was quite the opposite. And that rubbed him raw.

She emerged from her bedroom, looking every bit the

cool, reserved and well-heeled woman he'd met the very first day, only it was hard to forget that beneath that linen pantsuit was a body that made his teeth ache just to think of how it felt moving beneath and atop him. She had a lithe, dancer's figure with curves in the right spots and small, pert breasts that fit snugly in his palms.

It was a moment before he realized she'd begun speaking.

"I mentioned before that I don't do this sort of thing and I can only apologize for using you like that—"

His head whipped around. Using? Excuse me? "Come again, sweet?" he said, not quite sure he heard her correctly. "What did you say?"

Her expression appeared pained, even shamed, as she answered with pinked cheeks. "I'm sorry. That was insensitive of me. I only meant I was an emotional wreck over the confrontation I'd had with my father and I wasn't thinking clearly. And…it'd been a long time since…well, and you looked so…available…" She stopped, flustered by her mangled attempt at explaining the chain of events that led up to their banging boots, and honestly, he was still stuck on the part where she admitted that she'd used him for stress relief. "Oh," she said. "You don't have to worry about anything…I'm on the Pill and clean as a whistle. I assume you're also clean?"

Her brows pulled in a slightly worried frown, and he realized she was asking if he was free from any sexual disease. He tried not to be affronted; it was a logical concern when having unprotected sex with a total stranger, and he answered with a short nod. "Also clean as a whistle." He felt compelled to add that if he'd known he was going to be getting intimate he would've brought condoms, but that hadn't been his intention when Chick had put him in the room to wait for Emma. Or had it? It was pointless to try and say he hadn't noticed an attraction to the woman. Hardly. In fact, he knew he was inappropriately drawn to her almost immediately. But he hadn't known that she felt the same. "I don't make it a habit to have unprotected sex," he added stiffly. "Just so you know."

"Excellent. Neither do I. So we should be fine," she said, her smile brightening for just a moment as if a huge load had dropped from her shoulders. And it was disconcerting to know that *he* was that load. "Now, I'd appreciate it if we didn't speak of this to anyone. I'm feeling much more like myself this morning and I have a full schedule so if you wouldn't mind..."

Bollocks. She was dismissing him. To his recollection he'd never been dismissed in his entire life. And, as he shot her a dark look, he realized it didn't feel very good and he surely didn't want it to become a habit.

Perhaps he'd misjudged her response to him. Those breathless moans, the way her cheeks had flushed a lovely shade of pink when he'd teased and coaxed that sweet little nub of swollen flesh to a shuddering completion, or the wild, intense gaze they'd shared as they'd clung together, bodies working up a sweat as they'd brought each other to release multiple times.

No. He eyed her speculatively, shutting off the indignant male part of his brain and activating the former master interrogator. Even as she spoke, rapid with forced yet cheerful efficiency, her gaze darted to his midsection, bounced from his groin and avoided his knowing stare. He stifled a laugh. The woman was bluffing. Ah...two can play at that game. Suddenly he was intrigued by the challenge and accepted her silent invitation to play.

"You're absolutely right," he agreed, startling her with his easy acceptance. "Last night and this morning was an aberrant lapse in judgment that simply can't happen again.

I'm so relieved you realize this, as well. We can avoid all that emotional tediousness that always seems to follow these awkward morning-afters."

She crossed her arms but nodded as if in complete agreement while her mouth pinched and her gaze hardened. "I'm glad we're on the same page. We'll just forget it happened."

"Right. We'll just strike it from our memories."

"Of course." *Yeah, right. Good luck with that, sweetheart. You're already running images through your head.* He knew this because he was, too. "I can do it if you can."

She stiffened slightly. "No problem on my end."

"Fabulous," he said with good cheer, grabbing his jacket and slinging it over his shoulder. "So, we're good, then?"

"Better than good," she said, though her voice had lost some of its professional edge.

He stuck his hand out, and she seemed reluctant to shake it until she must've realized how that would come across. Finally she gave his hand a good, honest squeeze, and he returned it. As she pulled her hand back, he gave her palm a subtle caress that he hoped sent a shiver dancing down her back. She narrowed her gaze at him as if trying to ascertain whether he'd done it on purpose, but when his expression remained neutral, she backed down with a faint pull on her brows. Lord, she was a beauty, he mused as she walked him to the door.

"I'll see you tonight," he said, drawing a surprised look from her. He explained with professional courtesy, "There's still a killer out there, Ms. Vale—a killer who seems to have an obsession with Iris House. Until we figure out how to keep you and your boarders safe, I'm going to be your personal night guard."

"Oh," she said, drawing a short breath, distress evident in the fidget of her fingertips as she absently smoothed nonexistent wrinkles from her suit. "Well, if that's what you think is best," she murmured and glanced away, her gaze straying to the spot where they'd christened the floor before skittering away to focus on him again, her voice firming. "No funny business, Agent McIntyre. I meant what I said about the onetime deal."

"If you recall, you were the one who kissed me," he reminded her dryly then enjoyed the subtle flush in her cheeks as she did indeed remember that fact. "You have nothing to fear. I'll be the perfect gentleman."

The look she shot him either said *I don't believe you* or *I believe you and I'm disappointed.* He chuckled as he followed her out of the room. Either way, it ought to be entertaining to find out.

Emma couldn't get away from Dillon fast enough. She'd thought she had things under control, but somehow he'd turned the tables on her and she was left feeling as if she'd just lost a battle in a war she hadn't realized they'd started.

She suppressed a shiver as a memory assailed her mind of their naked bodies moving in tandem and nearly mowed Chick over as she hurried to her office.

"Where's the fire, turbo?" Chick asked, irritated as she nearly lost the stack of papers she'd been carrying. "I just got these papers organized and it took me all night."

"I'm so sorry, Chick," she said, smoothing the flyaway hair that managed to escape her French twist. "My mind was elsewhere."

A speculative look crept into Chick's expression and Emma nearly blurted *nothing happened!* which surely would've given away that something had indeed happened. It mortified her to her designer shoes that her best friend knew it. So before Chick could voice her suspicion, Emma moved forward as if nothing were different or unusual about her or the fact that the whole house knew Dillon McIntyre had spent the night in her room. "Are these the donation histories by donor and alphabetized by last name?" she asked, walking briskly to her office as Chick trailed her.

"Yes," Chick answered, closing the door behind her, causing Emma to frown as she took her seat at the desk. "Don't give me that look. You're going to tell me what happened last night."

Emma offered her best blank stare. "You're going to have to be more specific."

"Cut the crap, Vale. I can see right through you."

"I don't know what you're talking about."

"Bullshit."

"Paula," she said, using Chick's given name, which always served to communicate she was on the edge. "Language please. We have a teenager in the house."

Undeterred, Chick snorted. "A teenager who can outcuss a gangsta rapper on any given day. Now, my intuition tells me you're hiding something. Either you slept with the agent—which if you did I say it's about time someone knocked the rust off those pipes—or you had a fight with your parents and consoled yourself with a quart of Ben & Jerry's. So which is it?"

Not much of a choice. Perhaps she *should've* buried her heartache and soothed her temper with a quart of Chunky Monkey but she doubted her appetite would've been satisfied with a caloric overload. No, her hunger had been for something lean and muscled with a sexy accent. Good heavens, she had to flush him from her mind if she was ever going to pull off this balancing act. The fact remained that while she may have lied about wanting just the one-night thing, she'd been quite truthful in her belief that it wasn't in either of their best interests to keep tearing each other's clothes off. She suppressed another delicate shudder, and

Chick made a noise of exclamation that sounded a lot like a victory crow.

"I knew it!" she said, dropping the stack of papers with a dull thud to the desktop. Emma glared and she lifted her hands in surrender. "Listen, no judgment here. That guy is Grade A Choice for a Brit. I'll bet he has Scottish blood in him somewhere. Or maybe Irish. Anyway, no harm no foul. You were just getting your game on, and frankly, we all need to blow off some steam now and then, right?"

"Chick, please," she started, her cheeks flaming. "No more talk of rusty pipes, steam or any other metaphor for sex. I didn't—" She stopped before offering Chick another bold-faced lie, realizing it was pointless, and decided to go with honesty, embarrassing as the truth was. She sighed and slid the papers toward her as she fidgeted. "Well, I didn't *plan* to sleep with him, if you must know. It just happened and I feel wretched enough about it so if we could just drop it I would appreciate it."

"What happened?" Chick asked, ignoring Emma's request.

Emma discarded the paperwork for the moment and closed her eyes, but that was no use for there was too much imagery playing in her mental theater to find relief. She returned to the paperwork, determined to remain focused if nothing else. "I had a fight with my parents in front of Isaac. They want me to shut down Iris House because of this serial killer business and my father all but threatened to decimate our donor pool right before the Winter Ball. I came home upset and Agent McIntyre…um, well, he was available."

"Available?" Chick hooted. "So, you mean, he was willing to *service* you?"

"Oh, God, don't say it like that. Makes me feel like a Volvo in for an oil change," she grumbled, though if she recalled correctly that was sort of how she phrased it to

Dillon, as well. No wonder he'd been vaguely offended. "I wasn't thinking clearly and I took advantage of the situation. I'm not proud, so please…let's drop it."

Chick heard the plea in her voice and offered a short nod, even if there were more questions visible in her expression.

"Agent McIntyre has agreed we both suffered a terrible lapse in judgment and neither of us are looking to repeat it. That's why I just want to forget about it and focus on the things that need attention, such as these lists. We need to get invitations out by the end of the day if we're going to make our full capacity. We should've had them out last week. The caterer is already haranguing me for the final numbers."

Chick paused a minute, then said, "What if your dad makes good on his threat to shut down Iris House?"

Chick's question sat between them, and Emma wished she had a solid answer, but the truth was she didn't know what she'd do if her father pushed the issue. She hated to admit that he might have the power to do it, but then again, she couldn't pretend that his influence hadn't helped draw the wealthy benefactors to the seasonal fundraisers she organized to keep the house going. "I don't have a clue what I'll do. Not yet anyway," she admitted with a sigh, heavy with her own growing tension that everything she'd built might be destroyed. "But I'll figure something out. No one is taking Iris House down. Not my father and not some maniac," she said darkly.

She'd made a promise and she meant to keep it.

Chapter 10

Dillon stared at the intel he'd received through his cell phone from forensics on the paper the letter had been printed on. Here was something interesting, he took note, sitting a little straighter. The paper was high-end, not your ordinary stock found at the average office supply store. Forensics matched the paper to a store in New York that catered to society types for their customized stationery. Had the killer screwed up? Or was it on purpose? Considering that Emma traveled in tony circles, it might mean something. As if the killer knew Emma was accustomed to the best, which suggested he cared on some level for his target. Or that he cared for appearances.

Dillon considered all he knew of Emma and the boarders at Iris House. He still had to talk with Ursula and get her background, but last time he checked in she was still recuperating from the smack-down she'd gotten from her john.

He found it intriguing that Emma allowed Ursula to

hook and still live in the house. He could tell it bothered her even if she didn't say anything outright. He caught the worried expression, though she immediately blanketed it with a cool veneer. Why didn't she just insist that as part of the house rules the girl had to quit? It didn't make sense to him. It also didn't make sense why Emma was so driven to offer sanctuary to women who were clearly out of her social circle. Emma was uptown while the girls she fostered and protected were obviously downtown. Yet, she cared for them as if they were family. Perhaps he needed to dig a bit deeper into Emma's past to figure out the connection.

His phone trilled at his hip and after a quick check at the caller ID, he answered.

"Heard you were on a new case…kinda high profile," Kara Beauchamp said on the line. He broke into a delighted yet surprised smile at her voice. He missed his former partner but he didn't begrudge her a new life filled with happiness after the nightmare she went through during the Babysitter case. They'd all lost something in that case even if the bad guy, or woman was it were, was taken down in the end. "You doing okay?"

Her concern touched him but he covered with laughter. "What? Your husband doesn't keep you busy enough that you have to start poking around in my business?" he asked. "Being a mum isn't excitement enough?"

"Oh, it is and I love being able to be home with the kids. but I heard through the vine that you'd been assigned to a pretty big case and I was surprised and a bit worried," she admitted. "Last I heard you were content to stay away from the action. Now you're in the thick of it again with another serial killer."

He sent his gaze to the ceiling and scrubbed at his jaw, suddenly feeling every hour of sleep he'd lost last night while otherwise engaged. "Yes, well, things change and they needed someone with experience. I was the best man for the job."

He didn't say that they'd wanted Kara. She deserved peace after nearly losing her daughter, Briana, when the Babysitter, aka Crazy Wackadoo Woman, tried to even a decades-old score that she'd cooked in her head with Kara's kid as the bounty. The case had been national news because one of the Babysitter's victims had been the son of a California senator. Those days were hard to remember without some kind of flinch from everyone who'd made it out alive. "Last time we talked, you were having a bad time with the night sweats and nightmares. That all better?" she asked.

"Yeah, sure," he lied. He had a shrink. He didn't need another, and he regretted sharing that personal stuff with Kara, but he never imagined that this crap would still be kicking him in the tender parts each night. Besides, there wasn't much that could be done. He'd lost a team member during that case. It'd all happened so fast. He remembered two things: a dirty flash of white and Tana's expression of panic and fear a second before that. And then both he and Tana had been thrown out a window. For some reason, the impact had killed Tana instantly but he'd been spared. He'd spent a lot of time wondering why right after it'd happened. Now he didn't waste the mental energy on wondering but he still suffered the guilt. He forced a smile into his voice as he said, "Right as rain. Fit as a fiddle and all that nonsense." He paused and, though his heart ached to say it for he truly did miss her, he needed to get off the phone before she got him to remember too much. "I'd love to chat a bit but you caught me in a bad spot. I'll give you a ring when I have more time. Deal?"

"Don't make promises you won't keep, McIntyre" came her dry response, and he had to smile because she knew. "All right, you're off the hook for now. Just remember to stay tight and don't get hurt. I don't want to lose another friend."

"I rather like the idea of staying alive so no worries there," he joked but his palms had begun to shake. "Besides, this case is nothing like the Babysitter. I think I've already got this one figured out. No namby-pamby nursery rhymes to muddle through, you know."

"Thank God for that," she said but her voice softened as she added, "Don't be afraid to walk away. You don't owe the world. If it gets too hot, give it to someone else."

He agreed that he would even though they both knew he wouldn't. He couldn't walk away any more than she could have. Somehow the case felt personal for him. He couldn't fathom walking away from Emma, leaving her in the care of someone else…someone who might not know how to keep her safe.

But then, a part of him wasn't sure he was that man, either.

That saying about best intentions felt much too close for comfort.

But he wasn't walking away.

Not until the job was done.

And then? Who knows. He wasn't about to think that far ahead.

Emma was just leaving when Dillon returned to Iris House, something about his demeanor a little off. She hesitated, confused by her urge to inquire what was wrong and her desire to wipe away that look in his dark eyes. He was possibly the most handsome agent she'd ever seen—granted, her involvement with the FBI was fairly limited but even ones portrayed by actors didn't hold a candle to Agent Dillon McIntyre. She swallowed a distressed groan at herself and attempted to hurry past him but he stopped her with a frown.

"Going somewhere?"

"Out, Agent McIntyre. The needs of the house don't disappear just because of the current situation. I have errands to run, shopping to do and meetings to attend. Surely you don't expect me to hide in my room until this crazed person is caught?"

"There's an idea that has merit," he said, but she wasn't amused. The thought of remaining holed up in the house was enough to cause her to start chewing on her nails again, a nasty habit she worked diligently to erase from her early childhood programming. Seeing the set of her jaw, he said, "Fine. But you shouldn't go out alone. Take Chick with you," he instructed. "Or an agent."

"Chick is taking Cari to meet with potential adoptive parents for her child. It's a very important meeting and I wouldn't dream of asking Cari to reschedule just because you would like someone to hold my hand while I cross the street."

"And what about an agent?" he asked, ignoring that little bit of sarcasm.

She sighed. "The officer left around noon. And I was glad. There's something creepy about being watched, even if it's by someone who's supposed to be watching out for you. I'm just not accustomed to this kind of thing and it doesn't feel natural."

"Neither does being tied to a bed and assaulted and then sliced like a Christmas turkey," he said, shocking her with his plain talk of such gruesome things. She stared and he shrugged. "Sorry. But I don't seem to be getting through to you. There's a killer out there and that letter was addressed to you. In my experience, he's trying to tell you something. The killer wanted your attention. He didn't do that with any of the other victims. That tells me he's interested in *you*. Do you really think it's wise to make it easy for this person to snatch you unawares? He likely knows your habits, your schedule and is just waiting for the right opportunity. Don't make it easy for him."

She suppressed a shudder. He had a valid point. And she certainly didn't want to end up like Charlotte. She swallowed. She supposed she didn't have a choice. Emma drew a short breath and looked up at Dillon, resigned. "Would you mind accompanying me today on my errands?"

"I don't mind at all." He smiled and she forced herself to look away before she saw more than she was ready to handle. It was difficult enough to pretend that they hadn't been together last night—why she thought it would be easy was a mystery—but with him shadowing her every move it would be downright impossible. "What's on your agenda?" he asked solicitously, causing her to scowl.

"As I said…errands." Then a brilliant thought came to her. "Actually, I could use a male perspective. I'm planning to visit the caterer to discuss the menu items for the annual Winter Ball. It'd be nice to have a second opinion."

"My services are at your disposal."

She shot him a quick glance and when she couldn't decide whether there was some sort of innuendo hiding within the seemingly innocent statement she simply turned on her heel with an "I'll drive" thrown over her shoulder and a private prayer for strength.

Dillon supposed he hadn't planned to shadow Emma on her errands but when it became apparent she wasn't going to remain within the confines of Iris House until they could make arrangements for her safety, there'd been no choice.

She slid into the understated yet sleek black Mercedes sedan and he followed with a whistle of appreciation. She rewarded him with an arched brow as he admired the buttery leather interior inlaid with deep, rich wood accents that gleamed in the bright sunlight. "Gotta love German engineering," he murmured, stretching his legs in the roomy passenger seat. "But you surprise me. I would've guessed a sensible Honda for you. Something quiet, fuel-efficient and perfectly unnoticeable."

"How so?" She frowned, mildly affronted. "Are you saying I'm boring?"

"Not at all." Lord, help him, *boring* would never be a word he'd use to describe her. Sexy, controlled, hot, did he mention sexy? But never boring. "No, but seeing as you spend your time with…women of a certain nature, a Mercedes seems…"

"Ostentatious?" she supplied for him. When he didn't disagree, she simply smiled and brought the engine to life with the push of a finger. The luxury car purred like a content beast wearing a jeweled collar. "Agent McIntyre, I may spend most of my time with former prostitutes, but the people who help fund Iris House have lots of money and you can't circulate among those with money without showing off a little yourself. It's like your calling card. I consider the car a necessary tool in my arsenal."

"Smart," he admitted, resisting a grin of full-blown appreciation for her savvy, but it was hard. He respected that fully functioning, calculating mind. And damn if that wasn't a turn-on in the worst way. Sexy and brilliant. A winning combination by his estimation. "So does it work?"

The corners of her lips twitched, turning those luscious lips into twin halves of sweet temptation that he barely had the wherewithal to resist sampling. "Of course it does. I'm good at what I do," she said.

"I'm beginning to realize that," he murmured. "So what exactly is this Winter Ball you keep mentioning?"

"It's our biggest fundraiser of the year. As I mentioned, Iris House runs on the generous donations of others. Without it, we'd fold within a few months."

"How'd you get the seed money to start it?"

She slid him a sidewise glance, testing his reaction as she said, "My trust fund."

"Ah…" Vale Enterprises suddenly jumped to mind from the file on Iris House. He took a guess. "How'd the parents feel about that?"

"Not overjoyed." Her tone dulled but she shrugged. "It was my money to do with as I pleased. I chose to make a difference in the world rather than spend it frivolously."

"Some parents might find that noble," he offered for her benefit but she didn't seem to appreciate the sentiment. "So, what was their objection?"

Emma gave a short, dark laugh and shook her head. "Oh, just family stuff. They had different ideas about how I should live my life."

He mulled the small clip of personal information and wanted to push for more but he sensed her hesitance to discuss her family. She was intensely private, but he reminded himself that often what people sought to hide turned out to hold valuable clues to the puzzles he was trying to solve.

"So what compels a society girl to open a boardinghouse for prostitutes? Doesn't seem the kind of thing that women of your breeding are exposed to."

"Perhaps I'm not your average society girl, as you call it."

"That's apparent. But most people don't make overt changes to their comfort zone unless compelled to do so, either by some circumstance or situation, which leads me to wonder…what happened to you to make you want to buck what you've known your entire life, risking familial scrutiny in the process, to spend your trust fund on strangers and sacrifice yourself in the process to keep it going."

"Agent—"

"Dillon."

She shot him an exasperated look. "We've been over this. We agreed—"

"No, I never agreed. Call me Dillon," he said, wanting to hear his name on her lips at least once even if he knew it was inappropriate to encourage additional familiarity. But they'd already crossed the line…the damage was done, so to speak, so what the hell? When she pressed her lips together, he said softly, "Just right now. In the car. Where no one else will hear us. I'll call you Emma and you'll call me Dillon."

She faltered, shooting him an uncertain glance, then when he thought for sure she'd decline, she said, "All right…only in the car. *Dillon.*"

Chapter 11

Dillon took a moment to savor the small victory but there wasn't time to push his luck a further. They'd arrived at the caterers and she was already popping from the driver's seat, a bundle of efficiency in a soft linen pantsuit.

"Tell me about Robert Gavin," he said, surprising her just as she rang the doorbell to the restored Victorian. She gave him a quizzical look. "Do you like him?" he asked.

"Like him? He seems nice enough," she answered, still puzzled. "Where's this coming from and why now? Can't this wait?"

He shrugged. "Sure. I just wondered if you and him had a thing. And if you did, I wondered why you didn't know about his thing with Charlotte."

She stiffened. "There was no *thing* between Robert and Charlotte."

"You said yourself you didn't know why she had the picture of them together. Seems worth a mention seeing as everyone in the house seemed to recognize that he had a thing for you, even if it wasn't reciprocated."

"Will you stop calling it a *thing?* It's suggestive and misleading." Her cheeks heated and she seemed caught between embarrassment and indignation for his observation. She looked away as she answered. "These are questions best answered by Robert. I've never encouraged anything aside from a professional relationship with him. What he cultivated with Charlotte was ultimately his business not mine."

"But it bothers you that she didn't tell you," he pressed, eyeing her keenly. "I mean, you pride yourself on being the shoulder for everyone in the house. This seems like a pretty big omission on Charlotte's part. Did you express some kind of disapproval of a relationship on her part?"

She remained silent a moment, then deliberately pushed the doorbell again. "Charlotte's business was her own," she said. "That's all I have to say about that. If you don't mind, I have other things to occupy my attention."

"I'm not picking a fight." He wanted her to know, but somehow even as he said it he wondered why he felt the need to clarify. Maybe he was picking at something. It shouldn't but it bothered him that this Gavin character was free to ask her out like any other normal guy when he could not. He may have tasted and touched her body but he couldn't take her to dinner or a movie. The simple pleasure of a dating ritual was not available to him and it rankled. Why, he didn't know. Perhaps that's why he was out of sorts. The why of it was a distraction.

The door opened and a short, round woman answered and ushered them in with an exclamation. "I'm so sorry," she apologized in a rush as she led them to the back of the expansive home where the smell of something savory filled the downstairs. "I had the beaters going and didn't realize anyone was at the door. And you know, when I get to creating I lose all track of time."

"No worries, Samantha," Emma said with a gracious smile. "We were hardly waiting at all. Besides, I can't wait to sample whatever you have cooking." Emma turned slightly to Dillon, gesturing. "Agent McIntyre, I'd like you to meet the best-kept secret in the Bay Area. Samantha Grosjean, owner of Season To Taste. She's been the unofficial Iris House caterer for the past five years. I don't know what I did before her."

A delighted smile lit up Samantha's face and she blushed but her gaze fastened on Dillon with the same appreciation he imagined she bestowed upon perfectly prepared mutton chops. "An agent? Wow. I've never met an agent before. I mean, not a real one up close. Once I catered an event for the governor and I suspect there were a few FBI about but I never knew for sure...." She stopped as if realizing she was rambling and then launched back into business mode with a snap of her pudgy fingers. "Follow me! I have the samples out of the oven and ready for tasting. I think you're really going to love what I've put together."

"I'm sure I will. Everything you make is wonderful," Emma said, taking a seat at the high counter where plates of bite-sized portions awaited on pretty china. She eyed the plates and waited for the presentation. He took a seat beside Emma.

"I thought we'd start with grilled beef medallions served with port demi-glace or slow-cooked rib eye with pearl onion au jus and horseradish," Samantha said, pushing two separate plates forward with forks. "Don't hold back. I want your honest opinions."

Dillon doubted that. By the gleam in her eye, she expected praise and lots of it. But as he took an experimental bite of a beef medallion, he realized she expected it because her dishes were worthy. The medallion nearly melted in his mouth. He shared a look with Emma, and she rewarded him with a little smile, saying around a dainty bite, "I told you she was the best-kept secret."

"That, my dear, is an understatement. Not bad at all. What else you got there, love?"

Samantha tittered. "Oh, we're just getting started. By the time you leave you'll wonder how you ever survived without my cooking."

Dillon stuffed the last medallion in his mouth and then smiled around the bite, gesturing with his fork as he said, "Carry on then. You've intrigued me and I'm frightfully hungry. Oh, and love," he added with a wink, "might you have a good brew to wash it all down?"

Samantha giggled and dashed away to get him something yeasty to drink, and he turned to Emma, who was watching the exchange with something close to amusement and irritation, and said, "I'm so glad I came. I'd had no idea how I was going to talk you into supper. And here we are… dining together after all. Brilliant!"

Emma stared and ignored the flare of heat that kindled to life in her belly because she knew it had nothing to do with the spices Samantha used in her dishes. "This is not dinner, Agent McIntyre," she said beneath her breath, not wanting Samantha to hear their exchange. She loved her dearly, but Samantha was a bit of a gossip. She enjoyed hearing it and equally enjoyed spreading it. And Emma was not about to give her something to wag her tongue about, so she deliberately took another bite and chewed slowly as if this were an audition for service rather than a foregone conclusion that Samantha would get the job.

"How long have you known Samantha?" he asked.

"Five years." She spared him a short look. "She's not a suspect."

He ignored that. "Does she have any employees?"

"One. Jimmy and he's not your guy, either."

"Oh?" He pulled a small notepad from a hidden pocket on the inside of his jacket. "Let me be the judge of that." He winked. "It's what I get paid for."

"Jimmy is Samantha's son and when you meet him you'll realize why he's not a suspect."

"Appearances can be deceiving, Emma. You have to stop assuming—"

"Jimmy has Down syndrome. He's a lovely young man who helps with the table settings and buses the tables when everyone is finished. He is not a killer. He doesn't have a mean bone in his body. It's just not in his nature."

His expression was appropriately chastised so she let it go but she was weary of all his suspicions. She supposed it was natural and she should be grateful but she was unaccustomed to second-guessing everyone's motive. Frankly, she was ready for things to get back to normal. And, if she were being honest, she'd have to admit that it did bother her that she hadn't known about Charlotte and Robert, if such a relationship even existed. Why would Charlotte hide that from her? She'd never expressed any kind of censure to Charlotte regarding Robert, though if Charlotte had come to her she might have said that she felt it unwise to cultivate a romantic attachment to a donor as it could be misconstrued. Particularly so given the fact that the boarders of Iris House were former—or soon to be former—prostitutes. The whole thing gave her a headache. And she partly blamed Dillon for making her think of it.

They finished the courses—delicious as she knew they would be—and they left Samantha's, headed for home.

Dillon noticed her stiff demeanor and commented on it.

"Why don't you level with me and share what's on your mind?"

"That would take the rest of the night, Agent—" She paused when he reminded her with a pointed look of their odd little agreement. *"Dillon,"* she amended with emphasis. "But I'll be honest. I'm bothered by the fact that my life has been turned upside down and everything I've worked so hard to achieve is being threatened. It's hard to imagine why anyone would want to hurt me or my girls. Iris House was built with the sole purpose of helping people. Why would anyone want to destroy that?"

She hadn't meant to allow her fear and confusion to seep through to her voice, but it had and Dillon picked up on it easily. She sensed his desire to touch her, to reach out and comfort her in some way but knew he held back due to propriety, which she found oddly endearing yet annoying. She wanted him to touch her. She wanted to feel the soft rasp of his knuckles against her cheek or the caress of his palm against the nape of her neck. She wanted to march to her bedroom with him in tow, divest themselves of their clothing and lie snuggled together as if it were perfectly normal to do so. And that shocked her. She couldn't remember the last time she wanted that from anyone. It was as if there was a block of ice where her heart once beat and now Dillon's heat was causing it to melt. She concentrated on the road and clamped her lips tight so she didn't continue to spit irrational truths. Fatigue pulled at her and she still had a long night ahead of her.

"Tell me the reason you opened Iris House," he said, a subtle coaxing in his voice. The dark interior of the car lent a sense of privacy that encouraged her to share, even though she rarely talked about Elyse to anyone aside from Chick. "I know it must be personal."

"It is."

"Painful?"

She swallowed. "Very."

Silence followed and she knew he wouldn't stop digging. Eventually he'd find out, and she'd rather he hear it from her than some police file. Still, it was hard to talk about Elyse with a virtual stranger. She focused on the road, only instead of taking the road to Iris House, she detoured and headed for the hills. She didn't think she could do this without the buffer of the road. The distraction of driving enabled her to focus on the telling rather than the heartache that always followed.

"I was a twin," she said, hitting the freeway and leaving the city behind. If Dillon took note of her sudden detour he didn't comment. "Her name was Elyse. We were adopted by Veronica and Nigel Vale when we were born. Our mother was a teenage girl who wasn't ready for motherhood, much less twins."

"Was it an open adoption?" he asked.

Emma chuckled at the idea. Nigel Vale sharing something he'd bought and paid for? Absolutely not. "No. Elyse and I didn't even know we were adopted until we were fifteen. Elyse found the paperwork to our adoption when she was snooping in our father's desk for some cash."

"Ouch."

Emma's mouth twisted derisively. "Yeah. Ouch." She recalled the big blowup, the tears, the anger, the confusion. They'd clung together as they always had in times of crisis, but even so, Emma could sense the dark, yawning chasm that was swallowing her sister from the inside. That need to reconnect to the woman who had given them life and then walked away. Whereas Emma had thrown herself into her academics, Elyse had simply thrown herself away. Sudden tears pricked her eyes. "Elyse rebelled when our parents refused to help us find our birth mother. I think if they had, things would've ended differently. Elyse just needed to ask why, to hear that the decision had been made out of love not desperation."

"I imagine it was hard for your parents to accept that she wanted to know the woman at all. At that point they'd raised you, given you a home and a name…I can see how that would be difficult."

"My mom cried a lot. My father just got more bullheaded. He refused to help in any way and it drove a wedge between him and Elyse. Elyse started acting out in any way possible. It started with ditching school, dabbling in drugs, partying all the time, and then when our father cut her off from any funds, she turned to other means of supporting herself. She dropped out of school, ran away, and each time we brought her home, my father would try and force her to straighten up."

"How would he do that?"

She shrugged. "It varied. When she was still a teenager, he'd lock her in the house with hired guards to watch over her. Sometimes he'd lose his temper and hit her." That part she remembered with a flinch. Emma downshifted and pulled off on a secluded road. The lights of the city twinkled below them and silence followed when she shut off the engine.

"Was your father abusive often?" he asked quietly.

She considered that question. It was hard to answer. "I would say no but there were times…Elyse pushed him to the breaking point. And he left bruises. Afterward I would sneak in her room and spend hours holding her while she cried. I tried to talk sense into her, to get her to quit the drugs and the prostitution but by the end…she was so lost."

"How'd she die?" he asked.

Emma drew a breath to ease the tightness in her chest but it didn't help. Nothing did. Each morning she rose with Elyse's shadow, and each night before she fell asleep Elyse's last words followed her dreams. "A drug overdose. She was twenty-two." But by that point the drugs and the lifestyle had started to take its toll. Emma couldn't help but remember the sallow skin tone, the mottled and fading bruises each in various stage of healing, her thinning hair, the scarred-over pockmarks, and worst of all, the desperate soulless reflection in her blue eyes.

"Were you identical?" he asked.

"Yes." At least they'd been born that way. The differences were easy to see by the end. She shuddered and pushed the memory away. "She was my other half," she admitted softly. "Sometimes it feels as if she's still here…watching over me. But I know that's not possible."

Emma closed her eyes and startled when Dillon's fingertips grazed her forehead, pushing a stray lock of hair from her brow. Even though it was dark, she could almost picture those dark eyes softening with commiseration, as if knowing how difficult it was for her to speak so candidly of Elyse.

"Iris House is your chance to make it right for others," he surmised, to which she nodded with difficulty. "You couldn't save your sister so you're determined to save whomever you can."

"Yes." There it was. Out in the open. She rarely dissected her motivation but she knew deep down that's what it was even if she didn't share with others. "Now you know why I can't walk away. Why I will never walk away."

Dillon mulled over her admission before saying, "If it helps you heal from the loss of your sister it's a good thing. If it keeps you chained to a past you can't change, it's not. And only you know the answer to that. I say keep doing what you're doing until you figure it out."

Chapter 12

After they'd returned, Emma retired to her bedroom and Dillon took his post on the sofa, both dealing with what had been revealed in different ways. For Dillon, he'd been intrigued and saddened by the events that led to Emma opening Iris House, and her past led to a load of questions as well as gave insight to Emma as a person. But before he could delve more deeply into the side that he'd seen in the car, he had business to attend to and that took his immediate attention.

Early the next morning, he procured the house schedule, Emma's included, before heading off on his own errands. First up, he wanted a chat with Robert Gavin. The man was a loose end that needed tying before he could be written off as a suspect.

Dillon rang the buzzer to the exquisite multimillion-dollar Victorian, lovingly restored with no expense spared, and wondered if Gavin came from money or made it himself.

To his surprise Gavin answered the door.

Dillon flashed his badge along with a disarming smile. "Hullo, Mr. Gavin…I'm Federal Agent Dillon McIntyre. May I have a moment?"

The man, wide in the shoulders with a slight paunch and a chin that had started a slow slide into his neck, didn't seem surprised to see him. In fact, he seemed resigned, as if he'd known sooner or later some kind of law enforcement would come knocking at his door. *Interesting.*

"Would you like something to drink?" he asked solicitously as they walked into a formal living room, full of spindly French provincial furniture that definitely didn't look comfortable or picked out by a man's hand. Dillon declined and Robert sighed as he levered himself into a high-backed chair that was too girlie for words. "What can I do for you, Agent McIntyre?"

Dillon took a quick look around the room, his attention flitting briefly to a framed picture of an elderly woman wearing a stylish yet dated high-necked frock with multiple strands of pink pearls looping around her fragile neck and wondered aloud with a gesture toward the portrait. "Family?"

"My aunt," he answered, saying it like *ont* instead of *ant,* which Dillon found noteworthy. He filed away the information for later. "This is her home. She left it to me."

Dillon flashed a grin. "How nice of the old gal."

Robert smiled but it didn't reach his eyes. "Forgive me, Agent McIntyre…"

"I know, get to the point. Right. Were you in a romantic relationship with Charlotte Tedrow?"

Robert's skin tone flushed a dull red at the neckline and he stiffened a bit but he answered. "I suspect you already know the answer to your question, so ah, yes, we did enjoy each other's company from time to time. She was a lovely girl with a generous heart. I was distraught when I heard the news."

"And how did you meet?"

Robert paused a moment, a shrewd light entering his eyes. "Is this a formal interrogation?"

Dillon chuckled. "This is a polite inquiry, Mr. Gavin. An interrogation has a completely different protocol, in my experience. One that often involves pain and unfortunate instruments used with diabolical purpose." At Robert's widened stare, Dillon gestured. "Go on, you were about to tell me how you came to know Charlotte Tedrow before she died."

"We met at a charity event," Robert said, his lips tightening a bit.

"Oh?"

"Yes. The Iris House Winter Ball last year."

"That long ago? I find it interesting that Charlotte was able to keep your relationship under wraps from the house for an entire year."

"I didn't say that's when we became…better acquainted," Robert spat, momentarily losing his composure. "I said that's when we met."

"Right. Pardon my interruption."

"Charlotte and I started seeing each other casually—"

"Casually? Just to be clear, you mean when you became sexually involved?"

Robert's face reddened again. "Yes, if you must be so crude—"

"I must," Dillon said apologetically. "Just for clarification purposes in my own head. Go on, please finish."

"About three months ago. She was a lovely girl and surprisingly we had much in common in spite of our different backgrounds."

"Did you love her?"

"No. But I might have with more time," he admitted, softening for a moment. "She shone with an inner light that was simply alluring. I was mesmerized."

Dillon thought of Charlotte as he'd seen her, laid out on a cold coroner's slab, as far from a society girl as anyone could look, with her fried and overprocessed hair, scars on her arms from who knows what. He found Robert's poetic description a bit hard to swallow. Likely he was more mesmerized by her breasts than her personality. Still, Dillon wanted to see how far he'd take it. "Interesting. Rumor has it that you've had a thing for Emma Vale since you met. Was Charlotte a stand-in for Emma or had your affections changed?"

"I don't see how that information is relative to anything, Agent McIntyre," he replied coolly.

"Oh, you'd be surprised." Dillon smiled. "By your response I'd say you still think fondly of Emma Vale?"

"She's a fine lady. Who wouldn't?"

"Who wouldn't, indeed?" Dillon mused, mostly to himself. "But as I understand it, Ms. Vale has never encouraged your attentions beyond that of Iris House, correct? Does that make you angry? I suspect that'd make any bloke a titch annoyed. Good-looking woman, you a man of means…should be a match made in heaven."

"I think I've had quite enough of your *polite inquiry*." He stood and waited for Dillon to do the same. "If you wouldn't mind, I have things to attend to and I've just realized the time. It's been a pleasure," he said, his lip curling just a little.

Dillon stuck his hand out. "No worries there," he said good-naturedly, giving Robert's hand a hard, quick shake. "I've found what I need here. I'll be in touch. Don't leave town. I'd hate to have to chase you down," he said with a wink.

Dillon was barely out the door when it shut behind him.

That fellow wasn't very friendly. And he was plainly ashamed at having carried on with a former prostitute. No matter what he might've told Charlotte during their stolen interludes, he'd had no intention of squiring her about on his arm. Good for a tumble, not for a ring. Which meant he still had his sights set on Emma, because she was worthy of his economic stature.

So that told him Robert Gavin was a horny snob but it didn't make him a killer.

At least not on the surface. Dillon sent another look toward the house before walking to his car. Something about Robert Gavin made him want to look a bit deeper.

Emma was sipping her coffee when Chick came in, mad as hell and pulling a recalcitrant Bella along with her.

"What's wrong?" she asked, alarmed at Chick's actions.

Chick pushed Bella in front of her, earning a nasty look from Bella, as she said, "She's done it this time. And I, for one, am tired of trying to get her to clean up her act when she doesn't give a damn about how hard everyone around her is trying to help her. I'm done. She's your problem, Emma. I can't do it any longer. I'm sorry."

And with that Chick stomped from the room.

"That's one way to start a morning off on the right foot," Emma murmured, taking one last bracing sip of her coffee to savor the mouthful before she had to jump into the latest fray involving their youngest boarder. She laced her hands in front of her and looked Bella square in the eye. "What happened? And please, Bella, don't bother lying. We both know it's pointless because I'll find out the truth eventually anyway, and besides, I don't have time to deal with that right now. Just level with me."

"She's out to get me. She has been from the start," Bella said with an angry pout. "I didn't do nothing."

"Chick doesn't react without cause. What did you do? Something at school? Something here? Tell me, please, so we can find a way to fix it."

"Why do you care?" Bella shot back, her gaze darting from Emma to the floor. "Just kick me out and be done with it. I know you want to, and frankly, I'm tired of hanging around this dull place. No boys, no parties, no fun. I don't know why I've stuck around this long."

"Cut the crap, Bella," Emma said bluntly, not in the mood to coddle the teen at the moment. She had her own issues to deal with, and Bella's surly I-don't-care-about-anyone attitude was wearing thin on her already-taut nerves. "What did you do that was so bad that Chick is fed up with you?"

Mutinous silence met her question. Her jaw tightened. "Fine. Perhaps Chick is right. I can't continue to reach out to you when all you do is snap at me and anyone else who tries to help. I will find out from Chick what happened. In the meantime, go to your room and pack your things. I will call your social worker and give her the regretful news that you will no longer be staying at Iris House. You win, Bella. Congratulations."

Bella's eyes watered, but only for a second. Then she stuck out her chin and shrugged. "It was only a matter of time anyway. I knew it wasn't for real. I knew you didn't want me any more than anyone else."

"That's not true, Bella. I wanted you here more than anyone. But I learned a painful lesson a long time ago. People who don't want to be helped, simply won't be helped. Be ready within the hour, please."

Bella's lips thinned, but her brow dipped as if she were at war with herself, wanting to beg to stay, tempted to burn every bridge. Emma held her breath, hoping she would break down and ask to remain, but she didn't. She simply turned on her heel and slammed the glass door behind her, causing Emma to flinch.

Damn it. Emma cradled her head in her hands and fought the urge to pound her fists against her desk, frustrated and at her wits' end on how to get through to that girl. The fights at school, the ditching, the drugs, the parties, it was the same MO as Elyse before the big checkout. She swore she wouldn't let that happen to Bella. Somewhere deep down there was a sweet girl who just wanted to find her footing in a life that had nearly run her over at a young age. But Bella was fighting her every step of the way. Just like someone else had. Bella… *what do you need?* The question hammered at Emma, but all Emma received in return was a headache. Chick returned, a frown on her face.

"What now?" Emma asked, weary of the day when it had barely begun. "Is she up there breaking things?"

"No. She's packing. Are you really throwing her out?"

"Yes. Maybe you were right. She's a lost cause."

Chick looked miserable yet still pissed off. "Of course I'm not right. I never expected you to agree with me. You're the champion, I'm the hothead. Those are our rules. It's our version of good cop, bad cop. I tear them down and you build them back up again. It works. Now you're changing the rules midgame. What gives?"

"What are you saying? You said you were through. I figured it must've been bad enough for you to flip out on her. And she wouldn't tell me so I assumed you must've been right."

Chick cursed under her breath, muttering, "Well, it was bad. She broke a house rule."

"Drugs?" Emma held her breath, hoping it wasn't that. Anything but that.

"No. She sneaked a boy in the house last night."

The pent-up breath escaped in a confused whoosh. "A boy?" She hadn't expected that. Bella didn't like to be touched. By anyone. "How'd you find out?"

"I realized she was taking a lot of food up into her room and the kid hardly eats at all on a normal day. So first thing this morning, I went in there and he'd just slipped out the window. I saw his backside as he went over the side."

"Oh, Lord, was he hurt?" Emma envisioned a lawsuit if the kid broke something. "Where was I when all this was happening?"

Chick waved away her concern. "He's fine. He used the fire escape to shimmy his way down. But when I confronted Bella about it, she refused to talk. I tried to get her to open up, but you saw her—she clammed up tight. I just got fed up. She breaks the rules with impunity and never seems to suffer the consequences. I got hot under the collar about it and that's when I marched her in here, but I never expected that you'd throw her out. I was thinking you might scare her a bit and straighten her out that way. You know that kid isn't going to make it out there without some guidance." Chick stared, expecting Emma to make it right, and Emma knew with certainty that Chick felt terrible for losing her temper with the girl. Emma nodded and Chick's shoulders relaxed. "So you're not going to kick her out?"

"I should…but no. You're right. I do bend the rules for her. No sense in stopping now."

Emma rubbed Chick's shoulder on the way out and headed up to Bella's room.

She opened the door and found the teen packing slowly, as if she was hoping Emma would come and stop her. Damn if the child wasn't smart. Emma sat on the bed and sighed. "Okay. Who is he?"

"Who is who?" Bella hedged.

"I'm not going to play this game," Emma told her. Best

to be honest. Her nerves were frayed. "You know the house rules. By all rights I should stick to my original dictate and send you packing but if you tell me what's going on I'll see what we can do about the situation."

Bella stilled, her hands fidgeting with a folded turtleneck before dropping it in her suitcase. "He's no one."

"Is this how we're going to play this, Bella?" she asked, exasperated. "I'm trying to help you. I want to help you. All I've ever wanted was to help, but if you don't want my help, I'll stop. But let me tell you something…out there, outside of Iris House…no one gives a damn. I'd hoped after your time here you'd recognize the difference." Emma's voice was cutting but she couldn't help it. She wanted to throttle and hold the girl close but could do neither. She rose to exit the room but Bella's voice, tremulous at her back, stopped her.

"He's just a kid, like me. And he didn't have anywhere else to go."

Chapter 13

Dillon swung around the corner of the hallway and bypassing a drunk snoring off a bender in the corner, gave the apartment door two kicks with his booted foot. No way he was going to touch anything in this nasty place. Not even his knuckles to the front door. Dillon heard a muted crash, some cursing and then a bleary-eyed Mad Johnny opened the door.

"You again? What the fu—"

"Hey, watch your mouth…there are kids around here, you know. May I come in?"

Mad Johnny had the presence to give Dillon a dirty look then sneered. "You got a warrant?"

"Nope."

"Then piss off."

"There you go getting all surly and unfriendly-like. I'm just here to chat."

"I'm not in a chatty mood," Mad Johnny said, and then

tried to slam the door in Dillon's face, but Dillon anticipated that and put his foot between the door and jamb, then shoved the door into Mad Johnny's face, causing him to stumble back screaming something about his nose. "You crazy, mother… You broke it again!"

Dillon cast his gaze around the disheveled room before quietly closing the door behind him. Pizza boxes, flies and a putrid smell seemed to be Mad Johnny's decorating style. "You're a pig," Dillon observed casually, moving past the punk as he blinked against the pain and sucked back snot. "We have to talk." Mad Johnny shot him another nasty look that said *go screw yourself,* and Dillon saved him the time by saying, "Don't start with your mouth. I've come for some information and I think you might be able to help. Now, if you're wondering how I will be able to compel you to cooperate, I'll tell you because I'm feeling generous. You were one of the last people to see Charlotte alive. You were also blackmailing her with something to get her to do your dirty work. I want to know what you had on her. If you don't tell me I will make it my business to make your life miserable with frequent visits by police and I'm sure that will cramp your—" he glanced around at the pigsty Mad Johnny called home and then finished with a shudder "—style."

Mad Johnny tilted his head back to stem the trickle of blood leaking from his busted nose and wobbled to the equally vile kitchen where there wasn't a clean spot visible, grabbing a towel to mop up the mess on his face. He took his time in answering but Dillon gave him a little latitude. He wasn't heartless. He'd just broken the man's nose—again—for God's sake. A man had his pride. Even scum-sucking bottom feeders like Mad Johnny.

"What's in it for me?" he finally asked, his voice nasal and slightly muffled by the ugly towel pressed to his face.

"The ability to keep breathing," Dillon answered evenly.

"Right," Mad Johnny sneered. "There's rules even you have to follow. You can't threaten me like that."

To that Dillon just smiled and Mad Johnny visibly quailed. "Try me. Have I mentioned I'm a bit of a loose cannon?" He swirled his index finger around his temple. "Doc says my clock's not wound right." He shrugged. "Occupational hazard of dealing with scum like you and psychopaths on a regular basis."

Dillon held Mad Johnny's bloodshot gaze and finally the punk relented with a defeated shrug. "I got pictures of her doing some old guy."

"To run the risk of being blunt…so? She was a former prostitute. I suspect there are plenty of those floating around."

"Yeah, but this guy was real particular. She was afraid if he found out he'd dump her, and for some reason, Char had it bad for this guy. Once I realized she'd do anything to keep the pictures hidden…I knew I had her back."

"How'd you get the pictures in the first place?"

He smirked. "That was easy. All I had to do was slip the night desk guy a little cash and then set up a digital camera at the skank motel she and him liked to use for their little visits. Like I said…easy."

Dillon mulled over the information. "So, basically, you paid the clerk to give the couple whatever room you had rigged with the camera. What was in the package you had her deliver?"

"Do I get some kind of immunity for helping you out?" Mad Johnny asked.

"Sure," Dillon lied with a smile. "What was in the package?"

"Heroin. But it wasn't mine. I was just the middleman moving it around. Unfortunately, cops got my face on their radar and so I needed someone they wouldn't look twice at.

Since Charlotte started living at the group house, she cleaned up pretty good. I figured she'd get the package delivered no sweat. And she did. It went down smooth."

"Yeah, but then she ended up dead. Doesn't seem so smooth for her."

"Hey, I told you I didn't have nothing to do with that," Mad Johnny exclaimed, alarm coloring his voice until it got a little shrill. "She was fine the last time I saw her."

"So she did your little errand. Did you give her the photos?"

Mad Johnny's gaze skittered away. "No. I, uh, didn't get the chance."

"Yeah. Sure. My guess is you were planning to keep them for leverage. As long as she was seeing the older gentleman, you had something over her."

Mad Johnny knew Dillon nailed it. There was no sense in hiding it so he simply shrugged. "Yeah. So what? Business is business."

"Give me the photos."

"What?"

"You heard me. I want them. Now."

Mad Johnny swore under his breath, but he stalked over to a messy desk and after rooting around for a minute, accidentally knocking a half-full Coke bottle to the floor so that it fell and splashed all over his foot, he found what he was looking for. A CD case. "Here," he spat. "Everything's on there."

"And what about the original files?"

"Computer crashed and ate everything. This is it."

"Excellent." He pocketed the case. "If you're lying, I'll break something else," he warned, then smiled coldly. "It's been a pleasure."

"Are you going to keep showing up at my place?" Mad Johnny asked warily.

"Maybe. I find our visits…entertaining." Dillon paused at the door. "One more question… Did you happen to catch the name of the man Charlotte was seeing?"

"Yeah, some guy named Carlyle."

Dillon stared. "Are you sure?"

Mad Johnny nodded and pressed the towel against his nose. "Yeah, I remember because I made some wisecrack to Charlotte about her doing a guy with a sissy name. Then I asked her if he liked to wear her panties when she's spanking him."

Dillon's mind was moving in dizzying circles. Who was Carlyle? And what the hell had Charlotte been mixed up in? He patted the CD case in his pocket. Time to find a computer and take a look.

Emma blinked at Bella, shocked at the pain in the teen's voice. When Bella first came to Iris House she cared about no one and was strictly operating in survival mode. The fact that she felt compassion for a stranger was a huge milestone, but Emma had to consider the rules of the house.

"How'd you meet him?" she asked. "What's his name?"

Bella hesitated, biting her lip, clearly reluctant to share that information, which told Emma she was probably ditching school again. She withheld the sigh. *One crisis at a time,* she thought. Finally, Bella admitted, "His name is Ben. He was sleeping in the boiler room at school."

"And you found this out how?"

Bella cut her gaze away from Emma. "Because I go there sometimes when I need to get away from all the stupid people."

"Okay," Emma breathed, feeling a headache coming on. "We'll talk about that later. How do you know he's all alone? Is he in the system? Is he a runaway?" Bella's stony silence was answer enough. "Bella, if he's in the system, he has a home to go to. He can't stay here."

"He won't go back," she said. "Bad things were happening to him, Emma."

"What kind of bad things?" Emma asked, though she needn't have bothered. She could imagine. And when Bella gave her a hard look she didn't need to hear the details. Unfortunately, social services wasn't infallible. Sometimes a bad seed got through the checks and balances. "If someone was hurting your friend we need to alert the authorities."

"No one will believe him. He tried."

"I will believe him," Emma said firmly. "I will help him get out of a bad home but Iris House isn't the place for him permanently. You know that. It's a home for women only. It's that way for a reason." She frowned against the pounding gathering behind her eyebrows. "So, where is he now?"

Bella looked sullen. "I don't know. You scared him off."

"Well, you must know where he went?"

Bella shook her head. "He won't tell me. He doesn't want to go back to his foster family."

Lord help her. Emma took a deep breath, not quite believing what she was about to do. "When your friend returns…tell him he can stay until we get things figured out. But he can't stay in your room. He can take Charlotte's room until we figure out what to do."

"Really?" Hope, new and vulnerable, shone in Bella's eyes. "You mean it?"

"Have you ever known me to lie?" Bella shook her head. Emma smiled. "Well, I don't plan to start now. But this is temporary," she warned. "And if it turns out that Ben isn't living in a bad environment, he'll have to go back home to his foster parents. Do you think he'll talk to me?"

"I don't know…maybe."

"Well, tell him no one will hurt him here. This is a sanctuary, remember?"

Bella's mouth lifted in a sheepish smile. "I know. Thank you, Emma."

Emma reached up and gently moved a swatch of hair from Bella's eyes, almost holding her breath. When Bella stiffened but didn't pull away, Emma nearly sagged with relief. "You're welcome, Isabella." They shared a moment laden with tears that neither would shed at the moment and then Emma straightened. "From now on, no more secrets. All right?"

Bella bit her lip but nodded. "No more secrets."

Emma swallowed and savored the breakthrough. This was what she'd been working toward with Bella for the past six months. But as Emma left Bella's room, her buzz was short-lived. How would she keep her promise to Bella when the state would surely not agree to letting Ben stay if his parents wanted him back? She was skating along the edge of insanity. She should've flatly told Bella no. She had enough on her plate; she didn't need further complications. But she'd worked so hard to help Bella recover from the trauma in her life that Emma had nearly wept with joy at the appearance of compassion and empathy in the girl's emotional palette. She probably would've agreed to anything.

Emma detoured to her office, her mind in a jumble. She kept a board in her office with pictures of runaways; that way if she came across one, she knew the appropriate agency to contact. Sometimes kids ran away because their home lives were horrendous and the street seemed a far better option than living one more day under their abusive parents' roof. But other times, kids just ran away because they were young and immature with romantic delusions about life on the streets. Those were the ones who were only too eager to return to the comfort of their homes, their parents sobbing with relief as their wayward child was collected.

It was possible she'd missed a new runaway report with all that'd been happening lately. And it was possible no one had issued a report. The city was full of runaways; not every parent cared to have them back.

Where did this mysterious Ben fall?

Chapter 14

Dillon knocked on Emma's door, ready to start his night shift. Although his back twinged from being on his feet all day—another by-product of that lovely explosion—his mind was still chipping away at the mystery that had presented itself at Mad Johnny's and he was eager to ask Emma some more questions.

She answered the door and immediately his heart rate kicked up, setting his blood to percolate and simmer inside his veins. Even when she wasn't trying, she took his breath away. Wrapped in a soft gray velour tracksuit and fuzzy pink slippers with her hair tucked into a messy knot at the base of her head, she should've looked ordinary. In his eyes, she radiated beauty. Hell, she could've answered the door wearing a paper bag ensemble and his tongue might've still hit the ground.

"You look cozy," he observed, a smile warming his mouth as his gaze devoured her from head to toe. What would she do if he just pulled her to him and made love to her lips the way he wanted to do to her body? But as his feet carried him closer, obeying the growling hunger pushing him, the clear, agitated look in her expression stopped him. "What's wrong?"

"We had an incident with Bella," she said, her brow furrowing. He followed her to the living room, where she took a seat, kicking off her slippers to curl her feet underneath her. "Apparently she's been secretly housing a boy she met at school."

"Help me out. Why is this something that has you stressed out? I imagine teenage girls have been sneaking boys into their rooms for aeons. So, it seems she's normal. Isn't that a good thing?" he said, his hormones not quite ready to release his brain. Perhaps if she didn't look so delectable…

She gave him a look. "No one is allowed to bring home strays at Iris House. It's one of the rules."

"So you going to toss the girl out?"

"Of course not," she retorted unhappily. "While yes, she did break the rules, the very fact that she cares about another human being means she's reached a milestone in her recovery. So, I'm trying to help him in order to help Bella."

"Very noble of you," he said, taking a seat at the other end of the sofa, stretching out his long legs for a bit. "But I'm not surprised. You have a soft spot for the girl."

"Is it that obvious?" she asked.

"Yes, but that's all right. Everyone in this house makes special allowances for her."

"Oh, really?"

"Yeah, from what I can see, you and Chick protect her while the other ladies look out for her. She's their surrogate little sister it seems. Iris House is her family."

Tears pricked Emma's eyes and nodded. "It's true. I just never knew if Bella realized it."

"She does," he returned with easy confidence. During his interviews with the house, the common thread among them was their affection for the surly teen. He didn't blame them…he liked Bella, too. He'd always had a soft spot for the prickly ones. "So is he here now?"

She shook her head. "No. Chick scared him off. She only caught sight of him as he jumped out the window and shimmied down the fire escape. Poor kid must be so frightened out there. I wish I knew where he was staying just for Bella's sake. She's a wreck. This is the first time I've ever seen an emotion on that child's face aside from anger and contempt. I was so flabbergasted by the entire situation I might've promised more than I can deliver," she confessed, her distress pulling at him.

"Well, don't beat yourself up too much just yet. With everything going on right now, until we get a positive ID on this kid…I say let him keep his distance. Trust isn't something we can afford with that psychopath running around, looking for an opportunity."

"But he's just a kid," Emma protested.

"Maybe." He caught the unease fluttering between them. "And maybe…he's not."

Emma swallowed and rose sharply. "I feel the need for a glass of wine. Would you like some?"

"I suppose one glass wouldn't hurt," he said, and she was incredibly relieved. She didn't want to drink alone but her hands were shaking from the fear that had stationed itself in her stomach. She hurried to her kitchen and pulled a red wine from the rack without glancing at the brand or vintage.

What had happened to her world? She ran Iris House like a military vessel—efficient, orderly and structured.

This philosophy had served her well. Now everything was slowly unraveling, being pulled apart by a psychopath with an agenda only he knew. She poured the wine and a little sloshed out of the crystal glass. She bit back a cry of frustration. Jerking a paper towel free, she quickly wiped it up.

Drawing a deep breath to find some sort of calm, she scooped up the glasses and returned to Dillon where he sat, a pensive look on his handsome face. Somehow just having him here made her feel better, more centered. It was silly and rubbed the wrong way against her need for total independence, but she yearned to sit beside him and just relax for a moment.

She handed him the glass, which he accepted with a short smile that didn't bode well for a quiet evening, and she tried not to hold her breath in apprehension. "I know it's been a stressful day but I need to ask you some questions," he said with a look of regret. "It's about Charlotte."

She nodded and returned to her seat, longing to guzzle the wine in her glass rather than sip at it the way she was trained since she was old enough to socialize. "Did you find a lead?" she asked, ridiculously pleased to hear that her voice didn't wobble or quiver. An appearance of control would do in a pinch since she was dangerously close to revealing she felt the exact opposite.

"More of a curiosity," he said, earning a frown on her part. "I talked with that pleasant fellow Mad Johnny today. He was so kind as to share some new information with me."

Distaste pulled her mouth into a tight pinch. "He's a vile creature. I doubt he gave you anything of value. I might suggest a rabies shot if you got too close," she muttered, taking a deeper swallow of her wine, forgetting to let it aerate in her mouth. "What did he say?"

"Well, he was blackmailing Charlotte with some photographs of her and her lover, which I assumed was Robert Gavin—whom I also visited, by the way, and I found to be a total ass—but the man she was seeing was named Carlyle. Does that name ring a bell?"

"First or last?"

"I don't know," he admitted.

"Well, off the top of my head, I don't recall a Carlyle, though I suppose that's not a surprise. Charlotte wasn't required to tell me of her romantic attachments."

"Does it bother you that Gavin was seeing Charlotte sexually?" he asked.

She blushed a little and laughed, a trifle uneasily. "The easy answer is no but the honest answer is yes. I wouldn't encourage any of the Iris House boarders to engage in a sexual relationship with one of our donors. In my opinion, it sends the wrong message. I wouldn't want anyone to think that if they make a donation, they get personal favors. First and foremost, I have to consider Iris House and the ramifications of such a relationship, but then again, I can't tell my boarders how to live their lives. If one of them were to meet someone through their association with Iris House and it turned out to be the love of their life…who am I to stand in their way?"

"Well, let me set one thing straight…Gavin wasn't looking for true love with Charlotte. He was using her."

Robert? Kind, sweet, generous Robert? "How do you know this?" she asked, not ready to believe it. "Surely, he didn't just come out and say something so crude."

"Oh, of course not," he agreed easily. "At first he was congenial and suitably somber when the conversation turned to Charlotte, but when I questioned his relationship with her, he became more reserved…almost prickly."

"Perhaps he values his privacy," Emma said, still troubled by this new side of Robert she'd never even suspected. "It's not unusual or suspect that Robert didn't feel compelled to share private aspects of his personal life. It's simply bad luck that the woman he was seeing turned up dead."

"Perhaps," he mused. "But what if it's not?"

"Not bad luck?"

"Well, it was certainly bad luck for Charlotte but what if Gavin was actively hiding something? What do you know of this man aside from the fact that he's a generous donor to Iris House?"

Emma paused for a moment, thinking back, trying to remember when she first met Robert. He was a fairly new acquaintance introduced by another frequent donor…or was he? She frowned. "That's funny, I can't seem to remember how I came to meet him. I know it was sometime last year, but I can't quite recall who introduced us."

"How do you compile the guest list for the Winter Ball?" he asked.

"Invitation only. We make it that way so that it's considered prestigious to attend. We invite big money because we expect them to spend big money, either at the silent-auction table or with a straight donation."

"I'll need a list of your top donors," he instructed, at which she balked.

"That's confidential information. I can't just hand it over like a grocery list."

"It's not like that but if you need me to I could get a warrant," he said, watching as her lips tightened and her cheeks flushed with a faint dusting of agitated pink. She was circling the drain, he could feel it. Too many things were being wrenched from her control and it was like a sensory overload. "The information is safe with me," he promised. "I just want to check it over and run some names through the system. Something tells me we're dealing with someone who's accustomed to traveling in tony circles. He knows how to blend, how to move in and out of those circles without drawing attention to himself."

"But don't you think that it would be rather counter-productive to donate hundreds of thousands of dollars if you didn't want attention? We take a picture of the top donors to mount on a plaque for their contribution. It's one of our little tokens of appreciation. I can't see a killer wanting that kind of press."

"Unless he's a narcissist, which many serial killers are. They have no ability to feel empathy and often cannot think of others in relation to their actions. Their victims are simply objects used to fulfill their own twisted desires, whatever those may be."

"That's horrid," she said, shuddering. She finished her wine and contemplated another glass, needing the alcohol to blunt the razor's edge of worry and apprehension that cut at her ability to stay centered and focused. She stared at her empty wineglass. "Did Robert say how long he and Charlotte had been seeing each other?" she asked, privately mortified that Robert and Charlotte had been together.

"Yes, he admitted to three months, though I wouldn't put it past him to lie. He pretty much tossed me out as soon as the questions got too personal. But I sensed he was hiding something. And—" he paused a moment until she looked at him in question "—I think Chick was right…he has a thing for you."

Emma looked away. Damn Chick and her mouth. "I suspect he does," she admitted. There was no sense in lying. Robert hadn't been subtle in his pursuit no matter how much she tried to deter him. "I never encouraged him but I knew he hadn't given up."

"Out of curiosity…"

She cut him a sharp look. "Because I don't feel that way toward him. He's a generous man but not my type."

Emma tried not to see the way Dillon lost some of the tension in his shoulders when she answered. She wished someone like Robert was her type. He was stable, kind, patient...*dull. Where'd that come from?* She shook out the errant thought whispered in her mind and focused on Dillon. "But even if he'd been my type, I'm entirely too busy to casually date."

"Completely sensible," he agreed with a smile, but there was a glint in his dark eyes that sent a shiver down her back. "A woman in your position...dragging around a significant other doesn't seem your style," he said, moving toward her.

Her eyes widened, apprehension warring with her desire to meet him halfway, and she stammered as she tried to slide away, "Wh-what are doing?" By this point, he'd climbed her body, pressing against her in the most delicious way as somehow she'd ended up on her back, the forgotten wineglass leaving her fingers to roll harmlessly to the floor. "Dillon? We shouldn't...I'm not looking to date anyone, not even you."

"Shh," he instructed softly. He stared into her eyes, melting her with that heated gaze, demanding her full attention without saying a word. "Who said anything about dating?" he growled right before claiming her mouth in a sizzling capture that for a split second made her forget what she'd been protesting.

Why fight this? It's so good, a voice said in a breathy gasp that was surely not her own. There was a very good reason for not doing this. And in just a minute she would remember... any minute now.

Neither of them was looking for a relationship, but that didn't mean she was looking for casual sex. *Good God, no.* The idea made her feel dirty. She wasn't that kind of person and didn't want to be. And just like that the mental fog cleared.

She wrenched her mouth from his and gave him a hard push that toppled him right off her body.

"What the bloody hell, love?" he exclaimed, his brow furrowed in a dark storm of confusion and cooling ardor. "A simple no would've sufficed."

Emma sat up and crossed her arms, anger replacing the hot stuff flowing through her veins. "We agreed not to do this."

"We did?" he asked, indolently propping himself on one elbow. His tousled hair and reddened lips gave him a decidedly Lothario look that was incredibly sexy, but Emma sensed he probably knew this so she wasn't going to give him the satisfaction of reacting to it. He'd plainly gone against their agreement and was now feigning ignorance.

Sensing her patience was thinning with his act, he dropped it. "No, you made a dictate and I simply went along with it for the moment. But the fact remains that I find you incredibly sexy and you feel the same about me. We're consenting adults. I say we should let our feelings lead the way."

"Absolutely not," she snapped, incensed at how entirely *casual* he was about the fact that they'd been intimate. "That's not how I operate."

"And how do you operate, Ms. Vale? Educate me."

His request took her aback. "What do you mean?" she asked, exasperated. "I've already told you…"

Dillon pushed to his knees and moved toward her. "Yes, but the question is…did you mean it?"

She stared. "Of course I meant it," she shot back, though in truth she was a little confused at the moment. "I'm not a casual sex kind of girl. I'm sorry if I gave off the wrong impression."

He pulled back. "So you're looking for a commitment..."

"No, I'm not looking for anything."

Apparently he didn't believe her. "Everyone is looking for something, even if they don't want to admit what it is they want."

"You're talking in circles," she accused him, getting annoyed all over again. "I know exactly what I want."

Dillon's chuckle sounded dark around the edges as he said, "Love, wanting and having are two different things, aren't they?"

She fell silent. He was right. Privately, she wanted a life of her own. She wondered what it might be like to be less involved with Iris House, to have the freedom to explore the possibilities of a true relationship, but when she thought too hard about it, the inevitable conclusion was painfully clear.

It was either Iris House or a relationship, and she just couldn't make that choice. So it was better this way, to never know what could be. Besides, she was a practical woman and rarely prone to flights of fancy, so why did her chest feel as if something was sitting on it when she pushed Dillon away?

She stole a glance at Dillon and then scooped up her fallen wineglass. The whole thing was ridiculous. Him and her? A recipe for disaster. And frankly, she didn't need any more wrenches thrown into the cogs of her well-oiled machine. "Good night, Dillon," she said stiffly and then removed herself from temptation.

Chapter 15

Emma awoke with a stuffed-up head and a crick in her neck from sleeping oddly. Perfect, she thought wryly, wincing as she pulled herself from the bed. After last night she wasn't eager to face Dillon again. The man did terrible things to her resolve and she didn't know why she was drawn to him in the worst way.

Perhaps it was the darkness she sensed hidden behind that laconic smile and sharp gaze. He joked with his mouth but his eyes told another story. She'd yet to work up the nerve to ask him about the scar on his cheek. It was none of her business, really, she chided herself as she undressed and stepped into the shower.

It was hard to forget what she'd done in this very shower with Dillon. When had she become such a wanton woman? Taking her pleasure where she found it, even if she found it in the man assigned to her protection. Oh, Lord, she hardly recognized herself these days. It was likely the strain, she rationalized, but there was something she was hard-pressed to deny, lurking at the edge of her thoughts, reminding her that needs forgotten became needs unbridled.

She closed her eyes and tried to stop the memory of Dillon's hands on her breasts, his lips traveling along her flesh in a searing path across her collarbone, and the way he wrung wave after wave of cresting sensation from her body.

Get a hold of yourself, please. Not even as a teenager was she so hormonal. She cooled the water temperature, gasping as icy jets pelted her skin and sent all thoughts, aside from getting out of the shower, running from her mind.

Which is exactly what she'd needed to put herself on track.

Dillon made a quick call to the Bureau, patching straight through to the Internet Crimes division, where he knew he'd find an old friend.

"Jones," a voice on the other line answered. "What can I do you for?"

"IT geeks are bloody odd," he said with a grin, knowing his friend and former Child Abduction Rapid Deployment—or CARD as they called it—teammate would know right away who was calling.

"Hey, Dillon," D'Marcus exclaimed. "I wondered when I'd hear from you. Been a long time, buddy. How's it going?"

"Good," Dillon lied quite amiably. Really, what could he admit to in pleasant conversation? He couldn't say he was becoming infatuated with a woman he was supposed to be protecting and he'd made up the need to sleep in her apartment so he could be close to her and avoid his own empty condo. So he lied. "Things are excellent, actually."

"That's great, man. I was worried about you." D'Marcus's voice dipped low as if he didn't want anyone to overhear their conversation. "You know, after all that shit went down like it did with the Babysitter...I figured retirement was in your future. I mean, anyone would've folded up shop after what you went through. But look at you, back in the field, again. Talk about balls of steel, you crazy Brit. I love it!"

Dillon grimaced and stared at the ceiling. "Yeah, so I need your skills to help me out on a case," he said, wanting to talk business, not old times. He missed his old teammate but they'd both gone in separate directions since the Babysitter case. D'Marcus had taken a promotion to the Internet Crimes division on a different floor of the building and since they never saw each other, they might as well have moved to different states. But office gossip knew no floor boundaries and D'Marcus, being stationed in the hub of geek central, probably heard all the latest dirt on everyone. "I need you to run some names and check phone records. Can you do that for me?" he asked.

"That's child's play—you know that. Give me something I couldn't do in my sleep," D'Marcus scoffed. "Hit me with the targets and I'll have the info in an hour. What am I looking for specifically?"

"I want to get a snapshot of a man named Robert Gavin. His address is 343 Bush Street in Pacific Heights. He's some society tosser who may have a hidden agenda. I don't trust him. He rubs me wrong. I want to know what he buys at the grocery store, how much he pays for cable and what he puts on his credit card. Also, check his bank records for any large withdrawals or transfers."

"You got it."

"Thanks. Ring me if you find anything interesting."

"No prob. Good to hear your voice again, man. We should get together sometime, maybe get a beer or something real soon," D'Marcus suggested good-naturedly.

"Yeah. Good to hear you, too," Dillon said, his palms

starting to sweat. He rubbed them on his trousers. "Right, so I'll get back to you on that offer, yeah?"

"Sure. I'll call as soon as I got something worth talking about."

Dillon offered his thanks and then quickly rang off. Damn it. Wiping at the sweat dotting his brow he swore at his own issues. Get over it, man.

But before he could shake off the clammy feel of neurotic residue, his cell phone rang in his hand.

That was fast, he thought as he answered, believing it was D'Marcus again. But it wasn't.

"Agent McIntyre, we've got a problem," growled the man on the other end, and Dillon silently swore for not checking caller ID first. His new boss, Director Pratt, was nearly as difficult to stomach as his previous boss had been when he'd been with the CARD team. Dillon was starting to sense a pattern here. Perhaps he had a problem with authority. "I've got a complaint here by some scumbag with a purple Mohawk—"

"Actually, it's a faux hawk, sir," he corrected, knowing it would just further piss Pratt off. Damn, he had a bad attitude. It was a wonder he still had a job these days.

"I could give a shit," Director Pratt snapped, his voice raising. "What I do care about is the fact that a federal agent under my command is out there playing fast and loose with the rules. You broke his nose? Twice? Now this kid wants the Bureau to pay for the medical bills."

"The unmitigated nerve," Dillon said, glancing at his watch. He was supposed to meet Emma back at Iris House in a few minutes. He started walking to his car, dodging traffic while half listening to Pratt threaten him with suspension if he didn't straighten up and fly right.

"This isn't how things are done around here. You might've gotten away with a helluva lot when you were running around with that CARD team, but around here, we follow the book. You got me?"

Except when a friend needs a favor, such as when Nigel Vale placed a call and suddenly, all resources are directed toward the Iris House case when there were plenty of other cases needing attention, too. *Eh. Well, that was life.* "Right. Book. Anything else?"

"Don't patronize me," Pratt said, his voice lowering with barely contained anger. "I can tell the difference."

"It's the accent. You just think I'm being patronizing because my accent tends to make everything I say sound superior. I assure you…I'm not patronizing you, sir." *Yawn.* Perhaps Kara was right. He should've taken a longer break from the Bureau. Too late now. He wouldn't walk away from Emma. All jokes aside, he felt a growing sense of urgency to get this guy caught. "So this punk…did he tell you that he's a drug dealer and a pimp? Check his record. It's pleasant reading for a night at home."

"Be that as it may…the punk has rights. Stop stepping on them and we'll get along just fine."

"I'm trying to stop a killer. I thought that was the priority."

"Do it within the letter of the law. If I hear of anything else like this coming across my desk, you're off the case. You're trouble, McIntyre. I had my reservations putting you on point for this but your experience was supposed to make up for your bad attitude. So far, I ain't seeing anything for my investment, if you know what I mean."

Dillon clenched his jaw to keep from telling the man to go screw himself and while he was at it, screw his investment. Pratt was an asshole but he didn't seem to make idle threats and Dillon wasn't about to let Emma's case fall into the hands of someone else. "My methods may not be textbook but they get results. My conversation with that punk, Mad Johnny, revealed that the vic, Charlotte, had been having an affair with one of Iris House's top donors, Robert Gavin, though for some reason he went by the name Carlyle."

Pratt made some kind of grunt of approval. "Go on."

"Without the disc I 'borrowed' from Mad Johnny, we didn't have much to go on except my gut instinct that he was hiding something."

There was a long pause and then Pratt said, "All right but no more 'borrowing.' We need evidence that is admissible in court. Remember that."

"Of course."

And then Pratt was gone.

Dillon slowly pocketed his phone and blew out a long breath. Pratt was right. He was trouble. He'd wanted to kick that punk around. Hell, he'd been *hoping* for a little resistance so he had just cause. He'd always danced to his own tune but he'd also always tangoed within the lines. And then there was his attraction to Emma to contend with. He'd never put his personal feelings before a case. But there was something about Emma that made his pulse pound. He shook his head, caught between doing what was right and what felt good. Well, there was no hope for it. For the moment, he'd have to settle for that murky place in between because there was one thing he knew: he wasn't walking away. Not until he knew she was safe.

Chapter 16

Emma detoured toward Bella's room, her head pounding from not enough sleep the night before, and knocked softly.

A muffled answer to come in followed, and Emma opened the door, hoping to meet this mysterious Ben. Her hopes were quelled when she saw Bella studying quietly—and quite alone—on her bed. On one hand, Emma was ecstatic that Bella was doing her homework; on the other hand, she'd really wanted to catch a look at the boy responsible for making a change in Bella.

"Any visitors today?" Emma asked, taking a seat at the edge of the bed. Bella looked up and shook her head. "Oh. Can we talk a minute?" Emma might as well get this conversation over with. It was bound not to go well either way.

"Sure. What's up?" the teen asked, sitting straighter so that her back touched the headboard. "Something wrong?"

"Actually, well, I'm a little concerned about this boy. Now, before you get upset, let's talk this through a little bit."

Bella swallowed and something flitted across her features but she stubbornly held whatever it was back. "What do you want to talk about?"

"I checked the list of runaways and he's not listed. Are you sure he's who he says he is?"

"Of course I'm sure. Why would he lie?"

"I don't know. That's the part that worries me," Emma said, truthfully. "There are things happening right now that I don't understand the why of, but I can't deny are happening. Someone is out there, targeting Iris House girls. I have to be suspicious of everyone who isn't part of our 'family.' And that includes this boy. Please understand I will do my utmost to help him but I have to ensure that he's not a threat to the house."

Bella nodded slowly. "Okay," she said, her voice small. "Thank you."

Emma smiled. "You're welcome."

Now, she just hoped she wasn't making a huge mistake.

Dillon followed Emma into the office. "Everything all right?" he asked as she took a seat at her desk. She glanced at him inquiringly, and he added with a gesture, "You have that look on your face that says something is bothering you."

She arched one brow at him in amusement. "You know me so well that you can tell when something is bothering me?"

"I'm a fast study," he returned with a short grin. "So are you going to keep me guessing or are you going to share?"

She leaned back in her chair with a small sigh. "Perhaps later. Right now I want to know how much longer we're going to be under house arrest. The Winter Ball is this weekend and I'm up to my eyeballs in preparations. Not to be rude but you're slowing me down."

He surprised her with a laugh. "You know, I enjoy your candor. Not many people are so refreshingly honest."

She blushed a little. "Oh, God…that was so incredibly rude of me, wasn't it?" she asked, distressed. She fluttered her hands around her temple and massaged the skin. "It's been a day already and I'm quite worried about this situation with that boy. It gives me the creeps knowing he was sneaking into her bedroom at night."

"Did she tell you anything new?"

"Nothing specific but there was a vibe. Perhaps something she's holding back, afraid that it might color my opinion. You have to understand…Bella has had such a rough start. I can't stand the thought of someone trying to use that to their personal advantage."

"You really care about this girl," he said softly.

"I care about all the boarders at Iris House," she said.

"Yes…but Bella is special. Why?"

"I don't know what you mean," she said, skirting the question but the agitation was written all over her beautiful, expressive face. Dillon understood why Robert Gavin carried a torch for her. Emma opened her mouth to further protest but thought better of it and reluctantly confessed, "You're right. She is special. She reminds me of Elyse, which is probably why I first gravitated toward her but there's more to it now. I've come to…think of her as more than just another boarder who will someday move on. And that's terrible."

"Why is that terrible?" he asked.

"Because someday Bella *will* move on and I will have to be prepared to let that happen. She doesn't belong to me. She's a ward of the state. In fact, it's a daily battle to keep her at Iris House. Basically, I managed to talk her caseworker into allowing Bella to live here on a trial basis as part of a pilot program aimed at at-risk teens. But there are so many stipulations…and Bella isn't good at following the rules."

"A girl after my own heart," he murmured with a smile.

"Yes, well, they don't look too kindly on problem girls. I've earned more than my share of gray hair on that girl's account."

"So why not take it out of the state's hands?" he suggested.

She looked at him blankly. "What do you mean?"

"Formally adopt her."

Emma stared. "Excuse me?"

"Come now, you can't tell me you haven't thought of it before," he said. "Everyone can see quite easily that you love her like a daughter, even if, like you said, it started out as something else."

"It's not that easy," she said, closing her eyes briefly. "And you're right. The thought has occurred to me. I've even researched the process. I'm not eligible."

That he found troubling. He couldn't imagine a more loving person than Emma. "How so?"

"Dillon, do we really need to go into this right now?" she asked, clearly pained by it. "I'd rather not if you don't mind. Suffice it to say, it's not an option for me. Bella is not meant to remain in my care."

He wasn't ready to let it go, but he could tell she was teetering on the edge of tears and he wasn't going to be the one to push her over. He wished he could offer her solace by taking her mind off the problems facing Iris House and the threat of danger stalking her but he had nothing but more disturbing news to share.

"I took a look at the photos that Mad Johnny was using to blackmail Charlotte," he said, grimacing at the sudden tensing of Emma's shoulders. "They are of Robert and Charlotte. Trust me, you don't want to see them."

She gasped and her hand flew to her mouth. "What are you saying? Is Robert..." She couldn't finish and her face had paled. "Did he kill her?"

"I don't know. The pictures in and of themselves aren't indicative of guilt but I managed to procure a warrant. It was flimsy and it won't take long for his lawyer to rip through it, but at least we'll have the chance—however brief—to get a look at what he doesn't want us to see. I know this is difficult but I have to ask...did any of the other girls have a relationship of any sort with Gavin?"

"Not that I know of but I doubt that means much because I hadn't known about Charlotte and Robert." She sighed, then as a different thought came to her she sat straighter and narrowed her gaze, remembering. "I don't understand, I thought you said the man Charlotte was seeing was named Carlyle?"

"One and the same. Apparently, Gavin likes to role-play a bit. Plus he didn't want anyone to know he was hooking up with Charlotte so he made her call him by a different name. In case she talked no one would recognize him."

"What a pig," she said, glowering. "How demeaning to Charlotte..."

"I told you he wasn't interested in anything more than a tumble with that poor woman. I don't doubt he filled her head with lots of pretty lies but the evidence says otherwise. Be honest with yourself... Can you see Robert Gavin squiring someone like Charlotte to all the social events in town? She lacked finesse, poise and grace. She was a street girl and she looked the part. That's what he liked about her. It wouldn't have mattered to Gavin if she cleaned up, either. To him, she'd always carry the stain of her past. It also made it easy for him to manipulate her. Didn't you say that she was thinking of taking university courses in the next semester?"

"Yes, she was very excited about making a fresh start," Emma answered slowly. "Why?"

"The manipulative bastard probably dangled the carrot of respectability in front of her, implying that if she were a different kind of girl they might have a future together. All the while he kept her firmly on the street level by desiring the dirty girl."

Dawning came to Emma. "And because she wanted to remain with him she continued to play the part in the hopes of becoming someone dear to him eventually."

"Right. You deserve a gold star," he said with a faint smile. "Which is also why she was willing to do just about anything to keep those pictures from going to Gavin. She wanted to be the kind of woman Gavin would want on his arm, but if word spread that he was shacking up with a former prostitute… there goes his reputation."

"And there goes any hope of a future together," Emma surmised. She looked ready to vomit but she didn't sit there in a stunned stupor for long. She jerked open the front drawer and pulled out the guest list for the Winter Ball.

"What are you doing?" he asked.

She grabbed a fine-tipped pen from her tidy pen holder and purposefully uncapped it with a fluid movement before meeting his gaze. "Amending the guest list, Agent McIntyre. I've suddenly lost my affection for a certain person," she said icily, then deliberately struck Robert Gavin's name from her list.

Emma was shaking inside. Robert Gavin. Of all the horrible, despicable, wretched… She shuddered. And she'd allowed him to sit at her table, while laughing at his inane jokes. Oh, horror upon horror, she'd briefly entertained the idea of accepting his offer of a night on the town. "Do you think he killed her?" she asked, pausing a moment to look at Dillon. "Do you think it's him?"

"I don't know," he answered carefully. "I've got someone going through his phone records right now. The warrant should be processed by tomorrow. We'll know more then."

"But something tells me your intuition is saying he's not the one," she said, taking note of his closed-off expression. "Why?"

"Because men can be rutting bastards but that doesn't make them killers. And frankly, I don't see Gavin having the kind of mental agility that this guy has to pull off the murders we've been seeing."

"Damn. You're right," she admitted, but she was too incensed at Robert's duplicity to let it go entirely. "Still, one can't be too careful. Perhaps a cavity search is in order," she suggested, eliciting a rueful laugh from Dillon.

"From the pictures I saw…he might enjoy it."

"Oh, Lord," she blushed with a mild groan of distress. "I'm getting a mental picture and it's horrifying."

"Yeah, I felt the need to wash out my retinas, too. But you're right…we can't be too careful because even though I'm not sure Gavin is the guy…I'm not sure he's not. And I can't take the chance."

She replaced her list in the drawer and then tried to focus on something productive but her gaze kept going to the scar on Dillon's cheek. Her curiosity was an annoyance. She didn't want to know more about the man than was necessary. At least that's what she told herself with frightening regularity.

"Why aren't you married?" she blurted, stunned that the words had somehow slipped from her mouth with such a desperate ring. Heat crawled into her cheeks and warmed her entire face. "I'm so sorry. I don't know where that came from.… I'm not myself right now—" *Understatement* if there ever was one. If she started a list of all the uncharacteristic things she'd done since meeting Dillon McIntyre…well, she'd have a very embarrassing list.

"I never met anyone who made me want to be a better man," he answered, his gaze intense even if he was lounging in the chair across from her. "I'm a man with plenty of vices. Up until last year I was a chain-smoker, I drink too much and for very little reason, I find most people annoying at best, unbearably ignorant at worst, and I've been told I can be terribly rude without even trying."

She blinked at him. "Oh," she said, trying for a small smile as she asked. "Is that all?"

He shrugged. "If we're being totally honest, I've also been accused of being a bed hog."

Since they hadn't actually done any co-sleeping, she wouldn't know but she wasn't averse to finding out, she realized.

"You sound very disagreeable."

"Exactly. Now you know why I haven't married. Much to Mum's disappointment," he added in a surly grumble.

"I'm sure there's more to the story," she said. She wasn't going to point out that he was a handsome man—he surely knew this—and good-looking men didn't stay unattached for long unless there was some kind of truly fatal flaw. Although he'd been seemingly honest about his, she sensed a bigger reason. "How'd you get that scar on your cheek?"

He forced a smile. "It's not a very interesting story."

"Let me be the judge of that," she returned, using his own words.

"Well, perhaps I should've said, it's not a very *nice* story." When she remained silent, refusing to back down, he looked away but not before she caught the sense that whatever had happened had left more than a physical scar. "It was the last case I was assigned with my partner. You may have heard it on the news. The Babysitter."

"Oh, goodness, yes. That was awful. A woman killing children? I can't even imagine."

"Yes, well, she was quite the peach," he quipped darkly. "All because she lost her own baby. Frightening thought… her being a mother." He grimaced then continued. "In the course of the investigation we were following a lead and me and a fellow teammate, Agent Tana Miller, went into an abandoned old house only to be blown to bits by a homemade bomb the Babysitter left behind as a present. Tana was killed instantly. I recovered eventually."

"You lost a teammate?" Emma asked, sympathy softening her voice. "That's awful."

His tone roughened as he said, "Yes, well, terrible things happen in the field. It's a risk we all take. Tana was as good as they came. The Bureau lost a good agent that day."

"And you lost a friend," she surmised.

It was a long moment before he answered again, and when he did she thought she almost heard a catch in his voice. "Yeah…the entire team lost a friend. After that case, we all went our separate ways. Kara retired, D'Marcus transferred and Zane, well, he was never quite right after it all went down. He left the Bureau and I don't know where he went."

Emma stilled. There was pain there. Lots of it. This was the darkness she'd seen lurking under the surface of the irreverent jokes and biting sarcasm. Considering his mother was still in London, it was likely his team had become his family, which had become fractured after their teammate had been killed and the case solved. What a cost to bear. She reached out to him in the only way she knew how—in sympathy.

"I know it doesn't make it better and it's in no way supposed to be a trade, but I'm sure Tana would've wanted to do anything to keep that psychotic woman from killing another child…even if it meant sacrificing herself."

"How do you know that?" he asked sharply, though his eyes were sad. "She was young. Never married. She wasn't even dating anyone seriously at the time because she wanted her career to come first. Why her? Why not me?"

Ah, she realized with a small bubble pop of intuition. Survivor guilt. She knew there was little she could say that would be what he needed to hear, but she wanted to try anyway, if only to show him that he wasn't alone. She stood and came around the table to where he was sitting. He watched her approach, his gaze never leaving her. It was almost as if he were challenging her without saying a word, begging without moving a muscle.

"I don't know why it was her instead of you," she answered honestly. "Terrible things happen all the time and we don't always know the why of it. Please don't cringe when I say that everything happens for a reason." When his mouth tightened, evidence that he hadn't liked what she'd said, she continued undaunted. She knew that even as painful as it was to lose her sister, her death had been the catalyst to create something good in the world. "When Elyse died I didn't know how I'd get through it. I felt alone and adrift. My parents aren't the touchy-feely type. They don't give hugs or sympathy. They just march on. At least that's how it felt. It wasn't until recently that I learned maybe my perception of their reaction wasn't entirely accurate." She drew a deep breath, remembering her father's overbearing demands and her mother's fearful expression. Momentarily distracted, she refocused. "The point is, losing Elyse drove me to create Iris House in her memory. I help women like Elyse get back on their feet. But the truth is—and I'm not comparing Elyse to Tana—Elyse's dying…was probably a blessing. She was tearing our family apart with her drug addiction. I couldn't have seen that at the time but I do now."

"I don't believe in fate and all that rubbish," he said, his expression flat. "There was no good reason Tana died and I didn't. End of story. If believing that your sister died so you could start Iris House is the way you cope with losing her, fabulous. I just don't buy into that woo-woo New Age belief. No offense."

"Have you ever noticed that when people say *no offense* or *don't take this the wrong way* they are usually saying something that is either quite rude or offensive and likely to make the other person angry, hurt or defensive?" she asked, coolly. She was just trying to help and he was being downright nasty. Fine. She got the message loud and clear. "I'm sorry to have bothered you with my attempt at sympathy, Agent McIntyre," she said, moving to the door, intent on leaving him behind so she could clear her head. But he was there, having bolted from his chair as if he had rocket blasters cleverly installed in the heels of his shoes, and now he was hovering over her in the most disconcerting way. She attempted to back away but he was in her space. "Agent—"

"Dillon," he reminded her with a husky growl, his mouth moving ever so closer to hers, causing a shiver of anticipation to tickle her skin.

"What are you doing?"

"I don't know," he answered truthfully. "But I don't want to stop."

She inhaled sharply, intent on reminding him that this wasn't appropriate, and damn it, she was angry with him for being so closed off and uncommunicative—basically, for acting like every man she'd ever dated—but before she could get the words out, his lips were sliding over hers. Her knees trembled, threatening to send her dropping to the floor if he didn't catch her, and she forgot what she'd been planning to say.

That is until she heard a hissed "My God!" from the hallway and she realized they had an audience.

Robert Gavin, plump face turning red while his lips seemed to all but disappear as his mouth tightened with rage, speared Dillon with a look full of hatred and something else equally ugly as he said, spittle flying from his mouth in his delivery, "Your career is mine, *Agent* McIntyre," he snarled, looking briefly to Emma. "You can count on it."

Emma wasn't sure she could've said anything useful, her tongue was glued to the roof of her mouth from shock and mortification, but she'd also been a bit scared by the look of murder in Robert's eyes. If he'd had a gun, she didn't doubt the both of them would be sporting bullet-sized holes in their heads. "This is bad," she whispered, looking to Dillon to either put her fears at ease or confirm them.

She was hoping for the former but got the latter as Dillon's mouth turned down with grim acknowledgment. "Oh, yes. This is bad. I have to do some damage control," he said, grabbing his coat and slipping it on as he rummaged in a pocket for his phone. Once it was in his hand, he gestured to her as he dialed. "Stay put. I'll figure this out."

And then with the phone to his ear, he was gone as quickly as Robert, leaving Emma to wonder how the hell her world had gotten so screwed up.

Chapter 17

Dillon skidded into the director's office, knowing by the tic going off in the creases of the man's eyes that things didn't bode well for him.

"I can explain," he started, but he was cut off.

"I told you to walk the line," Director Pratt growled, slapping a folder on the desk. "What part of *walk the line* escaped you, McIntyre? English is your native language, isn't it?" He didn't wait for an answer to his sarcastic question and wisely Dillon didn't try to offer one. "There are rules for a reason. You can't go around doing whatever the hell you want just because you want to do it. You're supposed to be protecting Ms. Vale, not washing her tonsils. This is a serious breach of protocol. You leave me no choice but to pull you from the case."

Dillon tensed but fought to keep his cool. It wouldn't do any good to take a backhoe to the hole he was already knee-deep in. "Director, if I may...I'll admit kissing Ms. Vale was an error in judgment on my part but I think pulling me at this stage would be a detriment to the case. The Winter Ball is this weekend. I've been studying the donors and I need to see them face-to-face. It's my hunch that the killer is one of the people on the guest list."

"What proof do you have?"

"None yet, but I will. I have a gut feeling," he protested but Pratt waved him away.

"Sorry. We deal in hard evidence around here. You've lost your objectivity and we need a cool head. I'm putting Sanford on the case, effective immediately. That'll be all, McIntyre."

Dillon's skin pricked from the heat percolating from his temper and his growing fear that he'd royally screwed up and in doing so he just put Emma in real danger. Sanford was a decent agent but he didn't have the background, the intuition or the drive to ensure that Emma remained safe.

"This is a mistake," he said, his tone laced with steel. "Don't make—"

"No, don't you make another mistake," Pratt interrupted, his gaze hardening on Dillon. "I've got that Gavin man calling for your head, demanding that I can your ass over this situation. And even though kissing isn't grounds for termination, it sure doesn't look good. I have enough pressure on me with this case, so if you don't want to find yourself in even hotter water, you'll pipe down, realize I'm doing you a favor and just say thank you. You're no good to me, McIntyre. I had reservations about putting you on this case.... I can see now that I should've listened to my gut. Take the rest of the day off. And get your head on straight."

Yeah, sure. If it were that easy… As tempting as it was to continue to argue his case, he knew a losing battle when he saw it. Even though it went against everything in him, he forced himself to walk out the door and head to Sanford's desk. He stopped by his own desk and scooped his files, notes and miscellaneous items, and dropped them unceremoniously on Sanford's. "Seems you've been reassigned to the prostitute killer," he said tightly.

Earl Sanford—a man who thought he was slicker than he actually was, had a smarmy grin and drove a big, flashy car that was an obvious overcompensation for something—accepted the folder and leaned back in his chair to peruse the contents. "Tough break, McIntyre," he said. "Can't say I'm surprised. Word around the water cooler is that you should've gone out on a medical a long time ago. But I wouldn't worry about it. This case doesn't seem to be going anywhere. It's been weeks since the last dead prostitute popped up with the same MO as the last. Whoever it was has probably moved on."

That's exactly the kind of thickheaded thinking the killer was banking on, Dillon thought darkly. He hit Sanford with a mocking look. "I have a tendency to trash office gossip. Otherwise I might've been inclined to believe that you enjoy wearing women's panties and that you have a penchant for dressing in drag when you're in strange cities." Dillon paused a brief moment to enjoy the sickly blanching of Sanford's normally florid face and shrugged. "But like I said, I tend to ignore the stuff heard around the water cooler. And don't go soft, Sanford," he warned, all hint of mockery gone from his voice. This was serious and he needed Sanford to remember that. "We aren't dealing with your average dim-witted killer who slashes and runs. He's methodical and he's doing this for a reason."

"I don't need you to tell me how to be an investigator," Sanford retorted stiffly, casting a furtive glance around the room to see if anyone else had by chance caught what Dillon had said about the undergarments. "Anything else,

McIntyre?" which was code for *get the hell out* and Dillon knew it.

Dillon shook his head. He felt sick inside. If Sanford didn't end up with his throat cut, it'd be a miracle. He wasn't skilled enough to avoid a trap if the killer thought to set one.

For that matter, he hadn't been, either, and he was a better investigator than Sanford.

Bloody hell.

Dillon muttered something along the lines of "happy hunting," but he was already walking out the door before Sanford could respond.

He'd known he was slipping into a bad place when he couldn't get Emma out of his thoughts, but instead of pulling back he'd completely driven off the cliff and willfully allowed himself into her bed. After that, he'd known there was no going back.

His feelings were all twisted and tangled up in Emma Vale and he couldn't begin to know how to fix that. But the worst of it…he didn't know if he wanted to.

Emma pressed both hands to her cheeks and squeezed her eyes shut in some grasping hope of regaining her sanity. Robert Gavin had caught them kissing. She could almost hear the gathering storm awaiting her when this news hit the social circles. Some might titter at the gossip—which was harmless—but others might find it extremely distasteful and express those feelings by way of their financial donations.

"Chick," she hollered, needing to confess her fears to someone and knowing her best friend would gladly listen and perhaps even chastise her for her actions, which she certainly deserved. But as she rounded the corner she ran into Cari, who was leading with her rounded belly. She gasped and steadied the unwieldy young woman so they both didn't tumble to the floor. “Are you all right? What’s wrong? Is it the baby?”

Cari shook her head as she supported the weight of her stomach with her hand. “No, it’s Ursula,” she answered, distress in her tone. “She won’t open the door and I think she needs to go to the hospital.”

Alarm spiked through Emma, followed by guilt. She’d forgotten to check on the girl, assuming Chick had it under control. Grabbing her key ring with all the masters she rushed to the second level with Cari panting behind her in an effort to keep up. “When was the last time you spoke with her?” Emma asked, hurrying to Ursula’s door.

“Two nights ago. And then this morning I tried to bring her some breakfast but the door was locked and she wouldn’t answer. I didn’t think much of it until when I returned this afternoon and still hadn’t heard from her. I just have a bad feeling that she’s really hurt and nobody knows about it.”

Emma knocked once before saying at the door, “Ursula, I’m coming in. I need to know that you’re all right.”

Silence followed her declaration, prompting her to open the door.

She swung the door wide and saw the form of Ursula’s body lying in the bed, covers pulled over her head. The way her body was so still, made Emma stop Cari from running to her friend. “Wait,” she said, her voice strangled. “You stay here. No, on second thought, go get Chick.”

“But—”

“Cari…please, go get Chick,” Emma said, her voice thin but firm. Cari plainly didn’t want to listen, but in the end bolted from the room as fast as her belly would allow.

As Emma walked to the bed, she caught the faint scent of copper, and her stomach tightened against the fear. “Ursula?” she said softly, pulling the comforter gently from the young girl’s face. “Urs…”

The smell of blood became stronger but Emma couldn't see where it was coming from. Ursula's face, still bearing the purple-and-yellow marks from the beating she'd received from a john, was in repose, almost peaceful. Yet, Emma knew…

She pulled the comforter down farther and nearly screamed.

She'd found the blood.

And there was so much of it.

Dillon sprinted into Emma's office, where he found her, shaking, drawn, with her face puffed from crying. He'd barely beat the investigators there and even as he crossed the threshold, he could hear the opening and closing of car doors as they approached.

Emma looked up from the paper in her hand—he doubted she actually saw any of the words printed there—and he saw the tremble in her fingertips before she let the paper flutter to the desk.

"What happened?" he asked without preamble, knowing as soon as the agents got here he'd get punted to the side. Hell, he shouldn't even be here, but he couldn't let Emma go through this alone.

"She didn't answer her door," Emma whispered, shaking her head. "I went to check on her and…found her dead." Emma looked up, her eyes watering. "I should've checked on her sooner…I…"

He wasted little time in crossing to her and gathering her limp body into his arms. She felt boneless, though she clung to him. He murmured nonsensical words of comfort but inside his guts were churning. This was his fault. A voice at the door broke them apart.

"Ms. Vale, where's the body?"

Emma pulled away as if she'd been scalded and quickly

wiped away her tears. "I'll show you," she said, trying desperately to find that inner fortitude that she wore as her body armor. He knew he'd catch flack for it but he didn't care—he wasn't going to allow her to face this by herself.

He moved to her side in a silent show of support. Sanford's expression soured, but he seemed to catch from Dillon that getting him to leave would start a fight so he let it go. "After you, ma'am," he said.

Emma led the way, while Dillon and the rest followed. They went to the second floor and into Ursula's room, where the girl's body remained as part of an active crime scene.

Emma stopped short of the door, refusing to go any farther. "Is there anything else you need?" she asked, her voice strangled.

"No, ma'am. We'll take it from here. One thing, could you keep the boarders off this floor? We'll be here awhile processing the scene. But we'll do what we can to remove the body as soon as possible," Sanford said, showing sensitivity for the situation. Emma jerked a short nod and then fled the floor.

Dillon hesitated only a moment to speak with Sanford. "Listen, you and I both know even if I'm not officially on the case, I'm sticking around for Emma's sake. Someone has to look out for her during this investigation."

"Don't kid yourself, McIntyre. You're here for yourself. Now stay out of my way. I've got a case to solve," Sanford said in a quiet tone and moved past him to the room where Ursula lay tucked in her bed, slaughtered, while the rest of the house slept.

Chapter 18

Chick found Emma bawling in the supply closet, the one place she thought she'd find solitude in a house filled with Bureau investigators and frightened boarders.

Emma turned, still clutching a roll of paper towels in her hand, and then when she saw it was Chick, started crying all over again. "How did this happen? Someone sneaked into our house and did this horrible thing right under our noses," she cried, wiping at her nose with the wad of towels in her hand. It was her worst nightmare. Her sanctuary had been invaded. Her haven was contaminated. She always promised her boarders that Iris House was a place of refuge, but what now? What could she tell them? What would she tell her investors? She fisted the paper towels and stared hard at Chick, who had wisely remained silent. "What am I going to do about the Winter Ball?"

Chick, worry and concern in her eyes, simply shook her head. "I don't know. All I do know is you can't hide in a closet using all the paper towels," she said, causing Emma to nod reluctantly. There was logic there. She could cling to logic.

"You're right. I need to focus," she said, though her thoughts were still in a frightful mess. What was needed next? She looked to Chick, hoping she had the answer, which she did.

"There's nothing you can do for Ursula at the moment. You still have a houseful of scared boarders to deal with. The safety of the house has been compromised. We should look into private security at least for the next few days as a temporary measure. And you still have the Winter Ball to attend."

"I don't know. Maybe we should cancel," Emma said, worrying her bottom lip. Somehow it didn't seem right to throw a party when so many things had gone terribly wrong.

"We don't have a choice," Chick said. "You know the Winter Ball is the biggest fundraiser of the season, and I hate to say this but Ursula's tragedy might actually cause people to donate more generously."

Emma stared at Chick. "Oh, that's a terrible thing to say," she said in a tight whisper. "I wouldn't want people to donate just because of this situation. I want them…"

"You want them to donate and be generous in their donation," Chick reminded her, causing Emma to scowl.

"This just feels wrong," she said.

Chick sighed and took the paper towels from her. "Perhaps, but the long and short of it is if we don't get money rolling in, Iris House will close and all of your good work will wash down the toilet because all people will remember is that some prostitute got killed here."

Oh, God, Chick was right, Emma realized. She straightened and wiped at the remaining moisture on her cheeks. "You're right. The show must go on, so to speak. Thank you, Chick."

"No problem. Now, I came to find you for a reason."

"Oh?" Emma sniffed back the remaining tears in an attempt to regain her composure. "What is it?"

"Agent McIntyre is looking for you."

"I can't see him right now." She balked, actually retreating into the closet farther, as if she could snuggle in between the toilet paper and the napkins. "Tell him you couldn't find me."

"Why?" Chick asked, puzzled. "What's going on? I thought you liked him."

"What makes you say that?" Emma lifted her chin. "I don't know what you're talking about."

"Oh, come on. This is not the time for this bullshit. Whatever you're going through, get through it because there are bigger problems out there than whatever you two are doing, right?"

Shame flooded Emma. "Oh, Chick. What's wrong with me? You're right. I just don't know where my head is. All this sordid business has messed with me in the worst way. I keep seeing Ursula and Charlotte and I feel like my mind is about to break." She took a minute to slow down and think. After a deep breath, she asked. "Where is he?"

Only mildly satisfied, Chick said, "He's back in your office. Oh, and one more thing...if you're going to start something with the agent, then just be open about it. No one is going to crucify you for it."

"I'm not—" She stopped at Chick's raised brow and choked back her denial. She was wasting both their time by lying. But she certainly didn't know where she wanted to go with Dillon. All she knew at the moment was that she felt safe around him and that was something she wasn't ready to let go of just yet. "I'll think about it," she conceded.

"That's better than nothing, I suppose," Chick grumbled, then added, "now please quit hiding in the closet."

Emma nodded and moved past Chick. "I'll be in my office if you need me."

Dillon was itching to know what was being done upstairs but as much as he wanted to be a part of the investigation, he knew Emma needed him. Besides, he also knew he could get D'Marcus to let him in a back door to Sanford's files if he absolutely had to. For the moment, he wanted to make sure Emma was okay. She looked about to break, and who could blame her? Her world was falling apart one boarder at a time.

Emma entered the room, the only sign of the emotional upheaval in the slightly reddened tint to her eyes and the pallor in her cheeks. Otherwise, she seemed the same efficient and orderly woman he'd first met, ready to take on the day and deal with whatever was thrown her way—whether those challenges were dead bodies or difficult menus.

"Chick said you needed to talk with me?" She gazed at him expectantly.

"Are you all right?" he asked.

"Of course," she said too quickly. Total lie. But that was fine. Who would be okay under the circumstances? "If you don't mind I have to find private security for the house and make final arrangements for the Winter Ball...."

He perked up. "You're not canceling?"

"Of course not. We have obligations. I must see that this place doesn't succumb to the ugliness surrounding the house at the moment, and frankly, I refuse to let whoever is doing this ruin all the good Iris House has done in the past."

He admired her spunk, her courage. But the thought of her sleeping in the house set his nerves on edge. "Stay with me," he blurted out.

"Excuse me?"

Bollocks. He'd gone and said it. Well, it was out there now; he might as well run with it. "It's not safe here. Everyone should leave. I'm sure Agent Sanford has already suggested that everyone find a safe house for the evening. I'm volunteering my place."

"For all of Iris House?" she asked with a small smile.

"Well, I would but my apartment isn't large enough," he said, knowing he was completely bungling it. Oh, what the hell, if it got Emma out of this house he'd pack everyone into his apartment for the time being and figure out the details later. "But if the ladies don't mind taking residence on the sofa and overstuffed leather ottoman…"

"Rest easy, Dillon," she said. "We're not going to invade your inner sanctum. And we're not leaving our home. I'm going to hire some private security and we should be fine. Plus, I know the girls and I would feel very safe if we knew that you were here with us."

"You're asking me to stay even though I'm not on the case any longer?" he asked.

She smiled up at him with a hint of bashfulness that he found completely alluring. "I've gotten accustomed to having you around. And…I wouldn't mind if you wanted to…stay with me."

Perhaps it was the near-hysterical breakdown only moments prior, but Emma was feeling positively reckless. Chick had had a point back in the closet. There were bigger issues to contend with than their attraction to one another… at least for the moment.

"The thing is, I really don't think I want to be alone tonight. I'm trying to hold it together for everyone's sake, but honestly, what I'd really like to do is to go to my room, close the door and bury my head under the pillow for a few hours…or days."

"I don't blame you," he said. "No one would. And if they did, I'd have to do something drastically unpleasant to them."

A dark thrill chased down her spine, feeling as if his fingers had just traced the vertebrae, and she inhaled sharply. "You would?" she asked a little breathlessly before she recovered. "I mean, thank you but I doubt that's necessary."

"I'll stay," he said.

She nodded, suddenly shy, which was completely ridiculous considering she was a grown woman and certainly wasn't above enjoying herself in a man's company from time to time. But this felt different deep down in her bones. For a moment she wondered, if they'd met casually, perhaps over drinks or some other social event, would she have felt the same sparks and sizzles that she felt now when she was around Dillon.

Well, she supposed there was no sense in wasting too much time wondering, because they hadn't met under those benign circumstances and she had other things to occupy her mind for the time being. "I have to talk with the girls. They're very upset and scared. If you wouldn't mind…"

"I'll let myself out," he said. Then added with a grave expression, "But I'll be back tonight."

"I look forward to it."

And she did. Lord help her, she found herself breathing easier when only a few moments ago she'd been adrift.

Thankfully, she didn't have the time or the luxury of examining that fact for deeper meaning. She wasn't sure she was ready for the answer.

Dillon left Iris House and went straight to the house of Robert Gavin, where a team of agents were processing for evidence.

Gavin was glowering in the sitting room, a snifter of dark liquid clutched in his hand, as he watched the agents rifle through his personal effects. Dillon couldn't blame him for being a bit rankled, but he couldn't muster much sympathy given how Dillon knew the man had used Charlotte so grievously before she died.

To illustrate this fact, he gave Gavin a wide grin as he entered. "Perfect day for a search warrant," he said, taking pleasure in the way Gavin's face flushed a dull, angry red. "Why don't you save us all the time and effort and just tell us if there's anything we'll find that will help solve this case."

"This is harassment," he said.

"No, this is due process of the law," Dillon disagreed amiably. "But don't worry, we're pros at putting things back the way we found them."

A crash resounded in the hallway and Dillon winced theatrically. "Or was it we're good at breaking things? I don't know, I get those two mixed up. Either way, we'll find what we're looking for. I can promise if you had anything to do with Charlotte's death…we'll happily nail you to the wall, Gavin."

"My lawyer has advised me not to speak to the authorities at this time," Gavin snapped.

Dillon shrugged. "That's usually what most high-priced lawyers tell their guilty clients."

"I'm not guilty of anything aside from a predilection for experienced women."

"We'll see."

At that, Gavin barked a short laugh. "If you had anything aside from those damn pictures I'd be in custody. And as far as those go…there's no crime in what we were doing. And she liked it."

Disgust curled in his belly as he pushed the images from his head. The man was vile but was he a killer? Plenty of people were sick with their sexual fantasies but that didn't make them capable of doing what had been done to those girls. A growing sense of unease sharpened his voice as he said, "Shut it, Gavin. No one's interested."

"So how's it feel to be on the outside looking in?" Gavin asked, his tone losing its bluster and going oily smooth. Dillon cast him a dour look and he chuckled. "Get used to it. When I'm through with you, you'll be lucky to get a job working a toll booth."

"How touching. I didn't know you cared," Dillon retorted, not really worried about Gavin's threats. If he had a quarter for every time some asshole threatened his job...although it did sting a bit that he wasn't actively in the investigation because of what Gavin had told his boss. Still, he wasn't about to let Gavin know this. "Why Charlotte?" he asked, changing the subject abruptly to throw Gavin off guard. It worked for a second. Then a cruel look took over his ugly mug, and Dillon had to fight the urge to put his fist in it.

"She was easy to control," he answered simply, lifting his shoulder in a negligent shrug. "And she was wonderfully dirty. I like that in a girl."

"Not enough to admit that to anyone else."

He looked mildly appalled. "Surely not. She was a prostitute. Those aren't the kinds of girls you bring home to mother, so to speak."

"You're a pig."

He stiffened. "Let he who is without sin cast the first stone, Agent McIntyre."

"Cute. Quoting scripture. And a perfect one for someone who is a raging hypocrite."

"I didn't kill her."

Dillon cut away from Gavin, hating the uncomfortable resonance in Gavin's statement. He wanted Gavin for this crime but as much as he wanted it...it didn't feel right.

Suddenly, with a sinking certainty, Dillon knew they wouldn't find anything here.

But because Gavin was a bloody tosser, Dillon called out to the team, "Take anything of a sexual nature for DNA testing." He offered a mild, apologetic smile that he didn't feel in the least to Gavin. "We are looking for a sexual sadist. Gotta cover all bases you know. Cheerio, lad. I'll be sure to tell Emma everything we just talked about. Oh, and by the way, you're *uninvited* to the Iris House Winter Ball."

"That's not for you to decide," Gavin said between clenched teeth.

"Oh, I know. This comes from Emma herself. She thinks you're a vile creature and doesn't want you anywhere near her girls. Can't say I blame her, really. And if you have the bad taste to show up, security has been instructed to escort you out. Consider yourself warned."

And with that, Dillon let himself out. Crossing Gavin off the list of suspects only intensified the churning in his gut over the fact that the killer was out there, planning something terrible, and he had no clue how to stop him.

Chapter 19

Dillon returned to Iris House later that night, and as a force of habit, did a security check of the premises. Satisfied that there was no one lurking in hallways or broom closets, doors were locked and windows secured, he made his way to Emma's floor.

Emma answered the door, wearing a silken pajama set that was sexy and functional, much like Emma herself, and he lost the last bit of common sense he'd been holding on to.

He didn't waste time on pleasantries, just simply pulled her into his arms for a kiss that left no question as to what he wanted to do to her.

"Hello to you, too," she murmured against his lips. He shut the door with his foot and walked her to the sofa. He didn't want to talk. He wanted to touch and be touched. They tumbled to the sofa and Dillon nearly groaned from the pain caused by his straining erection. Her scent called to him, drove him crazy with need, and he wanted to feel the little shudders as she clamped down around him, tensing with small whimpers as she came.

There was an urgency riding him, perhaps it was fear, but he couldn't get her clothes off fast enough. He pressed kisses on each bit of exposed skin as he slid the silken bit of material off her shoulders and onto the floor. His clothes soon followed and they were skin to skin.

"So beautiful," he whispered against her rounded shoulder. "You haunt my dreams, you know that? Very naughty of you but I like it."

She gave a low, throaty laugh that was cut off by a sharp, delighted gasp as he sucked a rose-hued nipple into his mouth and suckled the sweet flesh until she twisted beneath him, arching with a moan and pulling at his hair. "No fair. I can't think when you do that," she managed to say right before he plundered her mouth again.

"Good. No thinking allowed at the moment," he growled. He couldn't wait much longer. He wanted to draw out her pleasure until she was mindless with it but he was fast losing control.

He hooked her legs with his arms and slowly pushed himself inside her, the sound of her quickened breathing nearly sending him over the edge. She lifted her hips and he went all the way to the hilt, closing his eyes as a groan escaped him. Everything felt so right…so good.

He slid in and out of her hot sheath, quaking with sensation as the tension built to a roaring need to spill inside her. He pumped harder and faster; sweat beaded their bodies as they worked each other, both moving unerringly closer to that final moment. He licked his thumb and found that tight, swollen nub nestled in the trimmed, dark blond thatch and helped her get there first. She shook beneath him, gasped his name and shuddered as she flew apart. He had little time before he came shortly after her, clenching sensation hurtling through his body as everything stopped—his heart included—and he collapsed against her.

It was several moments before either could speak. He rolled off her and tucked her into his side as they lay on the sofa, their breathing slowly returning to normal.

She gazed up at him and he gently traced the arch of her brows with his finger. Everything about her was delicate yet she was stronger than some men. "You're like a drug," she said softly.

"Is that a compliment?" he asked.

"I don't know," she admitted. "I just know that I don't have room for you in my life, but the thought of watching you leave makes me feel things I don't want to feel."

He nodded. "I take that as a compliment, then."

She laughed ruefully. "I don't know about that but I'm willing to let it go for now. I don't want to try and figure this out just yet."

That made two of them. Dillon gazed into her eyes and felt himself falling.

He'd never been in love before. He didn't know what it felt like, but if it felt like this he could imagine why so many people were always trying to find it. He'd fancied himself taken with Tana, but he realized there was a distinct difference between infatuation and that deeper emotion—the one that reached down into the marrow of your bones and imprinted itself in your very soul. Yeah…that was an accurate assessment of how he felt at the moment. But in spite of the warmth spreading from his heart to his entire body, he kept the revelation to himself. "You have the most beautiful breasts," he said, admiring the firm flesh with a grin.

"And you have the most delightful ass," Emma returned with a cheeky grin.

He continued his exploration, his gaze traveling to her stomach. "Your belly button is adorable," Dillon stated matter-of-factly. "And I get hard just thinking about those lips of yours and remembering all the things you can do with that mouth."

She blushed but she clearly enjoyed his perusal. "You're no slouch yourself with that tongue," she said in a husky whisper that sent sparks straight to his toes. He couldn't stop himself—not that he wanted to—and kissed her. As his lips meshed with hers, tongues tangling in a tender caress, he poured every emotion that he couldn't put to words into that kiss. The uncertainty, the exhilaration, the fear, the joy…he'd never known he could feel this way about another person, but with Emma wrapped in his arms, he knew it was real.

When he drew back, there were tears glistening in her eyes. Alarmed, he asked, "What's wrong, love?" She shook her head but her frown gave away her distress. "Have I hurt you somehow?"

"No, it's not you," she said, wiping at the sudden moisture trailing down her temples. "I'm just overwhelmed. The last time I felt this out of control was when Elyse died. I've structured my life so that I don't ever have to feel that way again, but now with you and everything happening around me, I'm lost and I hate it."

He understood, but it stung a little to be lumped up into the category of *inconvenient* and *messy,* particularly when he was poised to bare his soul. He shifted and gave her room to sit up and they both reached for their discarded clothing.

She slipped into her pajamas and then tucked her feet under her, wrapping her knees tight against her chest. "I can't choose between Iris House and you," she said.

"No one is asking you to," he returned quietly, struck by the irony that at the moment he may have found the woman he was in love with, she may love someone—or something—more.

"You're not asking me but it would come down to that."

"Says who?"

"Says me. Until you came along I was content to run Iris House and forgo a relationship. Iris House was all I needed. Now, I find myself yearning for things that are out of my reach as long as I have the house. I don't have a forty-hour-a-week job I can walk away from at the end of the night. The job is my life. I put out fires, I solve problems, I constantly have to be vigilant about fundraising because we are kept afloat year after year by donations.... How am I supposed to do all that and not expect that something would have to give?"

Dillon knew she was right. He'd seen it plenty of times in his career. To do great things, it took great sacrifice. He got it, and before now, he was a hearty supporter of the concept. But that was prior to suffering this infernal longing in his heart to have more with Emma. He wanted to tell her he'd never make her choose but eventually, he might. He knew that if it were in his power, he'd ask her to walk away now because of the danger she faced. He exhaled a long breath, hating the place they were in but not knowing a way out without causing damage to either of them. "You have to do what's right for you," he finally offered with a shrug, withdrawing. "I mean, only you know what that is."

She gave an unhappy sigh. "That's just it...I don't know. Iris House means everything to me. I don't even know who I am without it. This is my purpose, my dream. I wouldn't even know how to do anything different at this point."

"I get it," Dillon said sharply, then instantly regretted his tone. He couldn't fault her for her honesty, even if it hurt. But there was something he had to say first. "Iris House is a good place and you do amazing work, but maybe you should ask yourself how much of your self-sacrifice is enough? When will you feel ready to do something for you? When are you going to stop using Iris House to punish yourself for something that was never your fault in the first place?"

She glanced away, silent for a moment. When she did speak, her voice was strangled with tears. "She was my twin sister. It's hard to explain that bond. I should've been able to help her somehow. I failed. Do you know what it feels like to carry that around day after day?"

He did. It was crushing, but you had to keep on living unless you planned to climb into the grave with them. That was all he knew. Dillon's chest ached at the raw pain in her voice but he knew there was nothing he could say that would take away her burden. "She made her choice," he said. "And you have to make yours. That's all there is in life. There are no do-overs, no matter how hard we might want one."

She watched him as she asked, "Do you ever wonder what you could've done differently the day Tana died?"

His mouth tightened as bitterness washed over him. "Every day."

"So you know how it feels to live with regret."

"Intimately. But I can't change a damn thing about what happened that day. Tana died and the world lost a fine woman. She was one of the best. But she's gone. I deal with it, just like you have to deal with losing Elyse. The time is long past when you have to ask yourself 'what's it going to be?' and then resolve to live with the choice you make."

"It's not that easy, Dillon," she said. "You make it sound like all you have to do is pick yourself up by your bootstraps and soldier on."

He shook his head. "No…it's bloody hard, but it's what you have to do unless you're planning on checking out."

She inhaled a deep breath and dropped her head to rest on her knees. "All I feel is confused and scared," she admitted softly. "I wish I knew what the right decision was…for me… for the house.… I don't even know anymore. What I know is that there's more at stake than just my feelings. But—" She gazed straight at him and the intensity seared a hole into his heart as she said, "If it were just me and you and nothing else to consider…"

"Don't give a lad false hope, love," he said, turning away, hating how much it hurt to know that whether she knew it or not, she'd likely choose Iris House over anyone, including him. His mouth twisted in a sardonic grin. "It is what it is until it isn't, right?"

She bit her lip. "Yes, I suppose so."

Yeah…that's what he figured.

The night of the Winter Ball, Emma was a bundle of nerves. The guest list had dwindled and she had to wonder if her father had had something to do with it. He rarely made idle threats and if he meant to see Iris House shut down—on the pretense of protecting her—then he would find a way to do it. Especially since Ursula was found only days ago in the house. Emma suppressed a shudder and concentrated on being a gracious hostess on the outside even if she was a mess on the inside.

She caught Dillon walking the perimeter, looking sharp in his tuxedo, and she relaxed just a little. She hadn't realized a small smile had formed on her lips until someone commented on it.

"Now there's that beautiful smile I'm accustomed to seeing."

She startled and turned to see Isaac West standing with a warm smile on his face. Relief flooded her. "Isaac, I'm so glad you could come," she said, leaning in for a buss on the cheek. "I was so worried that my father had managed to convince you to put some distance between yourself and

Iris House." She was still mortified Isaac had witnessed the scene with her parents. She glanced around with a frown. "It seems he may have been able to convince a few…attendance is down."

He waved away her concern. "It's a down economy, but I wouldn't miss it for the world," he said then added gravely, "How are you holding up under this nasty business?"

She smiled nervously. "Fine, Isaac. It's a strain but Iris House will survive. We're made of strong stock."

"Of course. I heard about Ursula. Terrible shock, I'm sure," he said.

"Yes, it was," Emma murmured but left it at that. She got the impression Isaac was hoping she'd elaborate but she wasn't going to sully the night with talk of death and sadness. She forced a bright smile. "Tell me about your recent humanitarian mission? I didn't get the chance to hear about your ride on the elephant. That must've been terribly uncomfortable. So tell me, last I heard you were traveling to Thailand for something involving at-risk girls. Of course, because of my own work, I'm very curious about how it went. I've always wanted to open more places like Iris House—perhaps going international—but I seem to have my hands full with one."

Something dark flitted across his features but it was gone in a flash. So fast, Emma was sure she imagined it.

"Tonight is your night to shine, my dear," he said, laying a heavy hand on her shoulder for a brief moment. His touch was hot and clammy and made her want to step into the cool night air to remove the imprint. "I plan to make an extra-generous donation for your troubles as of late. You deserve only the best."

"It's all for the girls, Isaac. We appreciate your generosity. Please enjoy yourself," she said, noting Dillon's quiet stare her way. She sensed something was bothering him and offered a smooth lie to Isaac so that she could leave gracefully. "I see Chick trying to catch my attention. We'll talk more later. I promise."

"I look forward to it."

Emma moved as quickly as her clinging dress would allow and went to the hors d'oeuvres table, ostensibly to survey the selection, and Dillon followed suit as she knew he would.

He selected a plate and started mulling the choices of gourmet tidbits. "Who was that?" he asked.

"A friend of my father's, Isaac West. He's very generous and I'm relieved to see him here."

"I don't recall his name on the list of donors."

"Because he wasn't. He prefers his donations to be very private. You have to understand he's incredibly wealthy but he's very particular about where he chooses to share his money. He doesn't enjoy publicity, preferring to help in silence." Dillon's shrewd expression caused her to ask, "What? Surely you're not suspicious of Isaac West? I've known him for years. He comes from very old money. He's the kindest soul. He could never do the things that were done to the victims. Never. I'd bet my life on it."

"Let's hope it doesn't come to that," Dillon said darkly and she swallowed. "People rarely show their true selves to other people—particularly so of those who are psychopaths."

"This is supposed to be a grand social event but it feels like a funeral," she muttered, mostly to herself. "And please no talk of psychopaths. Someone might overhear you."

"You look stunning," he said abruptly, startling her with the change. Neither had had the courage to bring up the conversation they'd broached the other night, but the topic sat between them like a houseguest who had overstayed his welcome. She offered him a tremulous smile as she smoothed the black satin evening dress that slid along her curves to dust the tops of her sequined shoes. The snug halter top made the most of her breasts, which for the evening made her feel as if she were actually larger than a modest B cup. And that made her feel incredibly sexy. Well, that and the fact that Dillon's eyes were practically glued to her body. "That dress should be illegal," he said in a husky murmur that caressed her entire body.

"You don't look half-bad yourself," she said, pleased to note that her voice remained calm when inside she was starting to simmer with the desire to find a private, secluded spot with the sexy agent. She drew a short breath and smiled. "I had a feeling you'd clean up well," she said.

His mouth toyed with a grin as he said, "It's the accent. Goes well with a penguin suit." Sobering, he added, "Listen, I know you think I'm going overboard with the whole suspicious thinking but until I check out this friend of yours, I'd like you to keep your distance."

A spurt of exasperation almost had her arguing, but she recognized that he was just doing what was second nature to him and nodded. "Okay, that shouldn't be too hard. I spend most of my time circulating, anyway. But perhaps you could try looking a little less austere and a little more like you're having a good time."

He moved closer and she almost thought she could feel the heat from his body warming hers. "When you're safe, I'll relax. Until then…this is what you get," he said in a soft voice as his lips brushed the shell of her ear. Then he melted away into the crowd and she was left holding an empty plate and a heart full of aching desire that she could do nothing about at the moment but push it aside.

Dillon wished he could appreciate the sumptuous surroundings Emma had created for the upscale event. For all the bad things happening in the background of her life, Emma put on a seemingly flawless event. The caterers had outdone themselves on the food, the decorators had created an elegant theme and a jazz band kept the crowd with their toes tapping. Overall gorgeous—yet understated—and still, Dillon's skin itched with trepidation. He couldn't explain it. Kara used to call it her "gut" and she was never wrong. Dillon had never leaned too heavily on intuition, preferring cold hard facts to woo-woo rubbish but in the absence of evidence…he'd take anything he could get.

His cell phone vibrated in his inside jacket pocket and he found a quiet corner to answer it.

It was D'Marcus. "Hey man, I wanted to let you know that I found nothing of interest on that Gavin guy you had me run. Just your average high-society stiff with a secret penchant for seedy hotels and I'm guessing a little action on the dirty side."

"Perfect snapshot of Robert Gavin," he said. "All right. Thanks for the intel."

"You bet. I'm sorry nothing else turned up, man. Would've been nice if this case closed up neat and tidy."

"Wouldn't that be a sweet change of pace," he muttered, his shoulders tensing beneath his suit.

"Good luck with the case."

"Yeah…" He clicked off. He'd need it. They were back to square one with no suspects, and something told him…they were about out of time.

So lovely. So achingly perfect. He watched as Emma worked the room with effortless grace in spite of the turmoil in her life. She was his perfect woman. Anticipation slicked his palms as he took a measured sip of the aged whiskey, and he watched surreptitiously as Emma smiled and chatted, giving of herself so selflessly to a cause that was beneath her.

Tonight was the night he'd been waiting for, preparing for.

Everything had worked so well—almost synchronistically. It was certainly fate that was smoothing the way because they belonged to one another. One by one, the plans came to fruition as if by an unseen hand, guiding circumstance until he was within grasping distance of his perfect woman.

Nothing like the nasty, broken dolls he'd had to use for the past ten years. At first, he'd thought the revocation of his passport had been a condemnation of some sort from a higher power but then he realized it was simply a sign of better things right here on home soil. Just the thought of Emma in his possession, coming to him willingly, caused his shaft to harden unlike anything he'd ever experienced with the dolls. Sure, they served their purpose but it was so messy. The thrill was intoxicating. He rolled his shoulders and shifted discreetly before finding a refill on his whiskey.

Tonight.

Emma caught Dillon's furrowed brow and anxious stare, and she tried to get to him but Isaac West stopped her and she didn't want to be rude.

"Will the lovely Ms. Vale grant this poor soul a dance this evening?" he asked, the corners of his lips tipping up in an inviting smile. He extended his hand and there was no way she could decline without taking the risk of alienating her biggest donor to Iris House. She accepted his hand with a smile and hoped Dillon understood.

Isaac led her onto the dance floor where other couples were enjoying the music and was surprised when Isaac pulled her closer than normal. She laughed a bit nervously, saying, "Isaac, all the eligible ladies who've been trying to hook you for years will be jealous."

He laughed. "They don't hold a candle to the incredible Emma Vale. Have I ever told you that I've always held you in the highest regard?"

"Ah, no, but thank you for the lovely compliment. I think highly of you, as well. Your donations to the Iris House have made recovery and reintegration possible for many young women," she answered, drawing the conversation back to neutral ground. She'd never seen this side of Isaac and it was making her a little uncomfortable. She sent a silent signal to Dillon, who was trying to make his way to them, but the crowded dance floor impeded his progress. She smiled at Isaac but swallowed a lump of something that tasted like fear, though she didn't know why. "I knew from the moment my father introduced us that we would become fast friends. Your generosity—"

"Yes, I enjoy making a difference," he cut in, a touch of impatience coloring his voice for a moment, and his grip tightened on her. She stifled a gasp. "That's why I talked your father out of his fool idea that you should cancel the Winter Ball this year in light of the circumstances."

She forgot about her discomfort. "He told you he wanted me to cancel?" she asked, unable to disguise the hurt that radiated from his admission.

Isaac's gaze gentled as he said, "I took care of it, my darling Ms. Vale. He had the idea of coming tonight and making a scene but I persuaded him to see the foolishness of his plan. The embarrassment, the ridicule you would face…I couldn't abide such a display. In the end, after much discussion, he saw it our way."

"Thank you, Isaac," she said, struggling to keep her voice calm. Dillon was nearly there. "Iris House appreciates your efforts."

"It's my pleasure. You do such good work," he said, pulling her even closer until her chest pressed against his and she imagined he could feel the wild flutter of her heart as it banged against her breastbone in growing panic. "I've been thinking…have you ever considered opening Iris House to younger boarders? Let's face it, the odds of changing a person once they've reached a certain age are slim. Look at poor Ursula…still a whore even after all you'd done for her. Same for Charlotte. Both were still offering their soiled bodies to men for money. Shameful. But if you were able to get them younger…say twelve or thirteen, when they're fresh and their bodies are still ripe and firm, budding in their sexuality, you could help them to preserve themselves before they became as soiled as the older girls."

Emma wanted to vomit. She could feel the hard press of Isaac's erection straining against his soft trousers, and she was trapped in his arms as he talked with the soft fervor of a pedophile gazing at a children's catalog. First Robert, now Isaac? Had she been surrounded by perverts this entire time? *Dillon,* she wanted to scream, *where are you?*

And then, there he was. Smiling and tapping Isaac on the shoulder. "May I cut in?" he asked, his tone firm and brooking no argument, though Isaac clearly looked displeased to be interrupted.

"I suppose I mustn't monopolize the lady all evening," Isaac remarked, reluctantly releasing her. She had to make every effort to glide from one man to the next without running to the safety of Dillon's arms. Isaac smiled at Emma but sent Dillon a cool look before disappearing into the crowd.

"You're trembling," Dillon noted with concern.

"Just hold me," she managed to say before she lost her voice entirely.

"What did he say to you?"

"Nothing really…it was just the tone and the feel.… I don't know, I feel like I should shower. I'm sure it's just the events of the past few days that have me on edge but I felt like I was going to be sick. I've known Isaac West for years. He's never expressed an interest in me romantically, but tonight…I got the distinct impression… No, I must be wrong. My head is a mess. Now that I think about it, it's just silly. I'm so sorry. I'm overreacting."

"You should trust your instincts," he said, his mouth tightening with worry before his gaze returned to the crowd, suspicion in his narrowed stare. "Where'd he go? Maybe I should go talk to him."

"No, please don't," she pleaded with him. "I'm sure I overreacted. It's nothing. He's a wonderful friend of the family. I mean, he even persuaded my father to calm down before he came here and made a scene."

"All right, but if he comes around again, I want to be there."

She nodded her agreement and it took all she had not to lean into him in the hopes of absorbing some of his strength. She straightened with a deep breath. She was the hostess of the Winter Ball; she couldn't lose it right here in front of everyone.

"Is Bella here tonight?" Dillon asked, to which Emma shook her head.

"Because alcohol is served at the event, Bella has to remain home. She fought me on it but I had to stand my ground. Besides, she was hoping to talk with her friend Ben tonight. Apparently, we needn't have worried about the boy. He's back home with his real parents after I made a formal inquiry into his welfare in the social services system. There's been an investigation started on the foster parents, which makes me feel good. I have to tell you I was really stressed about the possibility that he wasn't who he said he was. This whole situation has me jumping at shadows in the hallway." She gave a short, rueful smile at the situation, but when she saw the tension on Dillon's face she swallowed with apprehension before she could ask, "Why? What's wrong?"

"I'm uncomfortable with Bella being at Iris House alone

given the circumstances. I think we should get back to the house. I have a bad feeling."

Just hearing him say that made her feel like something was wrong but she could easily chalk that up to agitated nerves. "If I leave everyone will know that something is wrong. I'll send Chick with you back to the house," she said, but he shook his head. She made a sound of exasperation. "Be reasonable, Dillon. This event is what keeps Iris House alive. Everything has to run as smoothly as it always does."

"Screw Iris House. There are bigger issues at stake here," he said tightly, and she couldn't help but react.

Excuse me? She stiffened. *Screw Iris House?* She glanced around, hoping no one else was listening to their conversation and said in a cool tone as she put more distance between them. "It may mean nothing to you but it means the world to me and my boarders. I'm sure everything is fine. Call me if you find anything of concern."

And then she left him behind.

He knew the minute she returned to the ballroom, her face pale but otherwise still as beautiful as she ever was—a true testament to her spirit, which he adored.

But as much as he wanted to admire her as she held court among the people clustered around her, he had work to do.

He was a patient man but he'd come to the end of his waiting.

Soon, dear heart. Soon.

Chapter 20

Bella awoke with a splitting headache and a knot on her head. Seconds later she realized she was bound and gagged.

Tears of panic squeezed from her lids and she tried to remember what happened. She was supposed to meet Ben at the corner but he hadn't shown up. She'd waited for fifteen minutes but just as she was about to turn back, a pair of hands jerked her into a van and something sharp had hit her in the back of the head.

She rolled to her side, wincing at the stabbing pain in her shoulders at the pressure, and narrowed her vision at the darkness surrounding her. Wherever she was, it smelled musty and old, filled with dust and neglect. An abandoned building or house perhaps. She was definitely lying on hardwood instead of carpet. Her ears pricked at the slightest sound as sweat trickled down her temple. A light flared from a lighter and Bella sought the source.

A man in a...*tuxedo* sat in a corner, smoking a cigarette. He inhaled deeply and blew it out slowly. "I knew you'd be a fighter. That's why I had to knock you out. Couldn't have you kicking and clawing, trying to get away. I don't like complications to my plans. And you're an important part of my plan. I'll be honest because I think it's cruel to give someone false hope—and I'm not a monster—but you're a loose end that will end up getting snipped because I can't afford to let you ruin everything."

She wiggled her fingers to see how much play she had but found whoever had tied her had done a pretty good job. Still, she slowly twisted her hands, working the rope until she felt the bite of it against her chafed skin. She ignored the burn and kept slowly working it as the man, whoever he was, continued talking.

"Don't get me wrong, I think you're beautiful. Even if you are a whore. I liked them all—Sweetie, Charlotte, even Ursula. Well, Ursula had a mouth on her. In the end, she was a liability. Have you ever watched a person die? Fascinating. Did you know you can keep someone alive for a very long time while inflicting a lot of damage?"

She fought back the urge to gag knowing that she could suffocate if she vomited.

"Too bad I couldn't take you with me," he mused, drawing on his cigarette. "You could be my daughter with benefits." He laughed at his own joke and then stubbed the cigarette out in an ashtray beside him. The small light afforded by the glow of the cigarette extinguished, and the room was returned to stifling darkness. "Stay put. The ball should be over soon and I've got a few things to do before we take off."

Bella heard his retreating footsteps and then a door closing behind him. She waited a few minutes and when she heard an engine starting and then the sound of the car driving away, she struggled in earnest.

If she didn't get loose, her life was over.

And she wasn't ready to die.

Emma's hand shook as she ended the call. Bella was missing. She didn't even try to hide the fear on her face as she made her hasty exit, giving short instructions to Cari before taking off.

The drive to Iris House felt like an eternity, and her thoughts kept her trapped in a level of hell that was nearly driving her crazy.

She should've canceled the ball. What had she been thinking? Now Bella was missing and she wasn't so naive as to think that this was coincidence. Someone had been watching and waiting for the right opportunity, someone with the resources available to him to accomplish this, and yet, she'd refused to leave the Winter Ball with Dillon.

Rage at herself for being so damn stubborn and clinging to something normal prevented her from keeping the tears at bay. She dashed at the moisture leaking down her cheeks and tried to stay focused on the road at the very least so she didn't end up kissing the bumper of the car in front of her.

She pulled up to Iris House and saw a familiar sight—agents and police tape. Ignoring all this, she went straight past the agent guarding the scene and went to find Dillon, who was comforting Chick, who was sobbing noisily all over his white dress shirt.

Chick saw Emma enter and immediately straightened. "Oh, God, Emma…he took her," she cried. "It was him and he's going to do terrible things to that poor baby girl if we don't find him first. He's a monster!"

Emma swallowed and looked to Dillon, whose expression

was tight and drawn. "What is she talking about, Dillon?" she asked, keeping her voice quiet for fear of screaming.

"There was a note slipped under the front door," Dillon answered as he walked toward her, steering her away from the forensics teams dusting for fingerprints. "Now before I tell you what the letter says—"

"Just tell me, Dillon," she cut in, her voice thin.

His lips compressed to a fine line and she knew whatever was about to come was going to hurt like hell or make her want to scream.

"He wants you to trade yourself for Bella."

"What?" She couldn't help but stare and think that perhaps she hadn't heard Dillon correctly.

"He says if you come willingly…Bella will walk free."

"Then let's do it," Emma said without hesitation.

"Hold on now, Emma," Dillon warned. "Before you get a false sense of hope, think this through. You know it's a trick. He's going to kill Bella either way. She's a liability. He's using your affections for Bella to get to you."

"I don't care," Emma said. "I can't take the chance that he won't hurt her if I cooperate."

"That's out of the question. I won't allow it."

"It's not your call. It's mine. Where's the agent in charge? I want to get this going. Where am I supposed to make the trade?"

Emma stared at Dillon through a wash of tears. She'd do anything to save her girls, but most of all, Bella. She hadn't plucked that girl from hell just to let her die at the hands of a psycho—not if she could do anything about it.

"This is my fault somehow," Emma said through the lump in her throat, reaching to caress Dillon's face. He started to protest but she shushed him with a shake of her head. "Maybe if I'd let her go instead of stubbornly holding on to her for selfish reasons she'd be safe right now. I have to do what I can to make this right for her."

"Not by bloody sacrificing yourself, you little fool," he said. "Think about it…Bella wouldn't want that on her conscience. We'll figure out a way to save her without sending you to the slaughter instead."

"These things never work out," Emma said, fear in her voice. "I'm not naive. I know that sometimes the bad guy wins and I can't take that chance! Let's make the trade, get Bella, and then I trust you will find a way to save me, too."

Dillon opened his mouth but closed it again, the wheels working in his mind even when he didn't want them to.

"You know I'm right," she said, using the momentum of her argument to push her point. "You have the best chance to catch him by using me as bait. As long as Bella is safe…I can do this. I *want* to do this. Please, Dillon…she means the world to me."

She stared up at the man whom she was giving all her trust, watched as he struggled with something she wasn't privy to, and then when he pulled her into his arms, she sank into the embrace, drawing strength for the fire she was willingly walking into for the sake of a girl she loved with all her heart.

Heaven help me. Let this work…

Sanford appeared in Dillon's peripheral vision and he bit back a swear word. He needed more time to talk Emma out of this idea. It was coming from a good place but he wasn't willing to take the chance if something went wrong. They weren't dealing with an amateur here. Likely, this guy had all the bases covered. And they were at a serious disadvantage because they still hadn't figured out who he was.

"Ms. Vale, may I have a moment?" Sanford asked, ignoring Dillon's hard stare.

She disengaged herself from Dillon and faced the other agent, a resolute look on her face. “I want to do this. I will consent to the trade.”

“Normally, I’d say let’s find another way—”

“We *will* find another way,” Dillon interrupted sharply. “This is a suicide mission and you know it, Sanford. I won’t sacrifice Emma for another.”

“We’re going to do our best to catch this guy before it comes to that, McIntyre. Don’t forget…we’re on the same side, right?”

Sanford was trying to calm Dillon down but it wasn’t working. Dillon’s heart rate was kicking up and he was scared. Damn it, he was the liability at the moment and he’d better get a hold of himself or things would only get worse. Dillon didn’t trust himself to answer so he looked away with a muttered agreement.

Sanford returned to Emma. “Is there anyone you can think of who might be obsessed with you? Anyone who made you feel a little off? Sometimes it’s the subtle things that we overlook that are actually a big help in putting the pieces together.”

Emma started to shake her head but then she shared a look with Dillon and he knew she was thinking the same thing as he.

“Maybe…well, it’s probably nothing but…tonight…Isaac West was acting a little oddly. He said a few things…” Her cheeks colored and she looked ready to backtrack but Dillon nodded in encouragement. She drew a deep breath and continued. “He said some things that made me uncomfortable. Something about the way he talked about young girls and then I felt his…oh, goodness…” She swallowed and her blush deepened. “I felt his erection when we were dancing.”

“Has he ever shown any kind of affection for you in the past?” Sanford asked.

"No, he's always been a perfect gentleman. I feel terrible for even suggesting he might be involved with this, but…I did feel uncomfortable with his behavior tonight." A sudden thought came to her and she visibly paled. "Agent Sanford, can you please check on my parents? Isaac said he'd spoken to my father tonight before coming to the ball and I'd feel better knowing they were safe."

"Of course. I'll put someone on it right away," Sanford promised, then turning to another agent he said, "Get me some intel on an Isaac West." He returned to her. "Listen, the exchange is supposed to happen at midnight. That doesn't leave us much time to prepare. We're going to put a GPS locator in your bra so that we know where you are at all times. Don't worry…we're going to catch this guy."

Sanford offered Emma a short, perfunctory smile that was probably meant to be reassuring, but Dillon knew Emma was shaking even if she was resolved to see this through.

"Tell me everything you know about Isaac West," he instructed her, needing to keep her focused as much as he needed the information to do his own investigating.

"He's like a member of the family," she admitted. "He's been a friend of my father's since I was in high school. When I opened Iris House he was always my biggest supporter. He always seemed so committed to helping our cause because his donations were always so generous. My father said he came from a monied family that went all the way back to the nobility of some kind. Beyond that I never thought to check."

"Why didn't he want publicity for his donations?"

"He said he didn't need accolades," Emma answered, her brow dipping in a slight frown. "At the time I thought it was so noble. A lot of donors enjoy the publicity because it feeds their egos, and I don't really care why they donate just as long as I can keep Iris House open. I guess I should've looked a little deeper. I should've been at the very least curious as to why he didn't want any publicity."

"This isn't your fault," Dillon reminded her, hating that defeated look creeping into her features. "This is the work of a madman. Stay focused. Now tell me more. Really reach into your memory. Did he ever have a relationship with any of the girls?" She shook her head.

Dillon speed dialed D'Marcus. The sleepy agent answered the phone. "I need you, Jones. Run the name Isaac West for me. It's a matter of life and death."

"Now I remember why I transferred out of investigations," D'Marcus grumbled, but Dillon could hear the man rustling around and a computer booting. "Got a DOB?"

"No, but he's an older man. Just run the name and see what pops up."

"Got it." A few seconds later, he said, "Man, someone is smiling on you tonight. I got a hit. Seems his passport was flagged for something. Looks like the Thailand government has filed a complaint for something but it looks like the case was washed. Does the guy have money?"

"Apparently lots of it," Dillon muttered.

"Yeah, well, he must've massaged someone's sense of duty with a lot of green. So in the simplest terms, no charges but his passport has been flagged."

"Got any addresses attached to that name?"

"Plenty."

"How about one for a warehouse?"

"No warehouses... Besides, he'd probably put a commercial property under a business name. What does he do for a living?"

"I don't know..." He turned to Emma, who was chewing her bottom lip with a worried expression as he talked with D'Marcus. "What does West do for a living?"

"Do?" She gave him a blank look. "He doesn't do anything. He's a philanthropist."

"Does he have a foundation or anything like that that he might use to funnel donations to charity?"

Emma thought for a moment and her face brightened. "Yes! West Ventures. That's the account he uses to write the checks to Iris House."

Dillon returned to D'Marcus. "Check out West Ventures."

D'Marcus came back with a surprised, "Yeah...I've got an address in The Avenues that, according to satellite, is an abandoned house on Springfield Drive. It sure doesn't look like something a millionaire would call home."

"It's worth a look," Dillon said. "Thanks, man."

"You bet. If I find anything else. I'll give you a ring."

Dillon went to find Sanford and Emma trailed behind him. They found the agent in the makeshift command center in the kitchen. He looked up as they entered.

"Good. We've got something," Sanford said, looking to them both. "Isaac West seemed clean as a whistle on the surface but when we dug a little deeper into his history we found some interesting things. Seems fifteen years ago he was a suspect in his wife's disappearance. A body was never found so the case was tucked away in the cold-case files, and I'm guessing because of his money and connections, the case was conveniently forgotten."

"I never knew he was married," Emma murmured. "I never even thought to ask."

"Likely he wouldn't have told you the truth anyway. The case wasn't local. It originated in Colorado," Sanford said.

Dillon turned to Sanford. "Here's something else. He owns an abandoned house on Springfield Drive under the name West Ventures. I think you ought to have someone take a look."

Sanford nodded. "I was just thinking the same thing. Anything else?" Dillon shook his head and Sanford snapped into action, leaving Dillon and Emma alone for the moment.

The midnight hour was approaching. He could feel the passage of time as if it were being scratched into his skin. Moving to Emma, he said, "Let's go upstairs and get you changed. As much I enjoy the view of you in this incredible dress…I think you might feel more comfortable in something a little less…revealing."

She seemed to have forgotten her attire completely, for when Dillon made mention of her dress, she actually glanced down and her eyes widened. "Goodness, you're right. I need to change. Will you walk with me?"

"Of course."

She offered a wan smile in gratitude and his heart contracted at the sight. He'd do anything to clear the pain and fear from her eyes and lift her spirits from the dungeon of black thoughts no doubt running around in her head.

Once upstairs, Emma disappeared into her bedroom and Dillon did a security check out of habit. After ensuring that no one was hiding in a closet or under the spare bed, he wandered to the window and peered outside. He saw nothing but total darkness. The absence of anything suspicious didn't settle his nerves. He knew until they had Bella and Emma safe, nothing would.

She came from her room and tucked herself into a corner of the sofa. Resting her chin on her raised knees, she looked young and scared. Dillon went and sat beside her. He wasn't sure what to say or whether she wanted to hear anything so he simply offered her quiet companionship. He wanted to tell her he knew this waiting was a special kind of hell. He understood her pain and would do anything to take it away.

He hoped she knew that but he didn't want to burden the moment with unnecessary words between them.

But it was Emma who spoke first. "From the moment I first met you, I felt something for you. It was something I didn't want to feel or acknowledge, but it was there. I'd like to say that it was simply circumstances that pushed me into your arms that night but I think I might've ended up there eventually. I've wanted you from the beginning."

In the face of that stark honesty, Dillon responded in kind. "Everything you just said, I felt the same. You knocked me over with your grace and quiet beauty and I don't regret a minute spent with you." He took her hand in his and searched her sad blue eyes. "But why are you telling me this now? Is this a goodbye? Some kind of closure in case things go bad and you don't come back?"

She looked away and answered in a whisper. "Maybe."

He pulled her to him and she went willingly. "Stop. We're going to figure this out. Don't start saying your goodbyes. I'm not ready to hear them."

She snuggled in closer and clung to him. He realized as he stroked her damp hair and murmured soft words of comfort against her crown, he might never be ready for goodbye. Not from her. Not ever.

And the realization did nothing but make him want to bundle her up and take her far, far away, even if she fought him tooth and nail, because the thought of her in danger made his heart pound with fear and he couldn't stand it.

But because he couldn't do what he wanted to do, he simply held her and hoped for a miracle.

Chapter 21

Bella pulled her wrist free, biting back the groan of the excruciating pain caused by the constant grinding against the rope, and wiggled her other hand free. A rush of blood to her extremities felt like daggers poking at her but she had little time to cry over the pain. She ripped her gag free and as quickly as her wrist would allow, she managed to untie the knots at her feet. Kicking the rope loose, she froze when she heard a noise at the back of the house, her heart leaping into her mouth as the unmistakable sound of footsteps came her way. Inching her way up the wall, she tried to find something to use as a weapon. Her grasping fingers stumbled on something hard and she picked it up. It felt like a brick or a rock of some sort. It would have to do, she thought with desperation.

A bobbing light, consistent with an electric lamp, came her way and as she recognized the man, she swung as hard as she could, smashing the brick into the side of his head before he even knew she was hiding against the darkened wall. He fell with a strangled yelp, and Bella bolted from the room, blind and lost, but she followed the way she'd seen him coming from. She saw a door and ran for it. She slammed against the door and twisted the door handle only to find it locked. *God, no,* she thought in blind panic. *Help me!*

A fist grabbed her by the hair and jerked her away from the door. She managed one good scream before he cut off her airway with his forearm.

"You shouldn't have done that," he said against her ear as she struggled to get free but his grip felt like iron across her windpipe. "Now you're going to have to be punished. Say nighty-night Baby Bella.... Daddy is going to put you to bed."

Bella struggled as he dragged her away from freedom... away from her chance at getting out of there alive, but her strength wasn't enough to overpower her attacker and she squeezed her eyes shut against the fear pounding behind her breastbone as she fought for each breath.

Emma was dressed and ready. Dillon seemed ready to kill something. She tried not to look his way. She didn't want to chicken out. Bella needed her. They'd find a way to save them both.

As they entered the kitchen, Sanford and his team were heading out.

"What's going on?" she asked in alarm, her worst fears coming to roost in her head. "Is it Bella? Oh, my God, it's not time yet for the drop-off!"

Sanford stopped her, saying, "We've had a disturbance call in the Springfield Drive area. San Francisco P.D. reported a woman screaming. Our guy out there heard it, too, but needs backup. We'll call if we find anything. Until then, stay put."

Emma swallowed but nodded. "Please let this be the break we need," she whispered as the agents filed from the house and took off. She looked to Dillon. "I'm so scared."

"It's going to be all right," he murmured, though his expression said something different, and she had to hold back a frightened sob. What if they didn't find Bella in time? Maybe she ought to go to the drop-off spot just in case the disturbance was unrelated. Her thoughts must've scrolled across her face for Dillon shook his head. "Don't even think about leaving. You're going to stay put even if I have to sit on you. You're safer here."

"What about Bella?"

"We have to trust."

"I don't have the luxury of trust right now," she retorted bitterly.

"I know," he acknowledged with a grim set to his jaw. "I know."

Isaac dropped Bella's limp body to the floor and hastened to the window. He swore under his breath when he saw cops approaching. The bitch's screams must've caused someone to call the authorities. He glanced at Bella with regret. He'd been looking forward to playing with baby Bella. But he didn't have time any longer. His plans were ruined. Time to reevaluate. But he wasn't worried—he had a contingency plan.

He slipped out the back door and disappeared into the night.

Although the agents were gone, there was a uniformed officer keeping watch outside. Dillon was upstairs checking the windows and doors and Emma felt the overwhelming need for some tea.

Returning to the kitchen, she had only just put the kettle

to boil when she heard a strange sound. She turned but saw nothing. Still, shivers caused goose pimples to riot across her forearms until she rubbed at them vigorously. She was jumping at the slightest sound, she thought darkly.

Upstairs she could hear Dillon walking across the hall, checking with each boarder, and she smiled at his diligence. As she turned to grab a mug, she came face-to-face with Isaac West.

She opened her mouth to scream but Isaac pulled a black snub-nosed revolver from his jacket pocket. He pressed a finger against his lips as he pointed the gun right at her heart. "Shh…mustn't wake the others. It's been a very busy night," he said with the same warm smile she'd come to know from him, but suddenly it took on a totally different context. His smile no longer appeared warm but sickly and twisted. "I will kill you if I must but know in my heart of hearts, killing you is not my desire. You're different from the others. The one I've been waiting for. I'd hoped you'd come to me willingly but I see now that others have prevented you from doing so. Come, my lovely, we've a plane to catch."

"I'm not leaving with you, Isaac," she said, trying for calm. "Where is Bella?"

"She is safe," he answered. "Come, I will take you to her."

"Where?" she asked, buying time. "Tell me where she is so I know she's safe. She's just a child, Isaac. Surely you don't want to hurt a young girl."

He scoffed gently. "A child? Hardly. The moment she allowed men to pay her for sex she ceased to be a child, my dear. But that's what I love about you. The ability to see beyond a person's flaws to the beauty beneath. That's how I knew we'd be perfect for one another. As you may have discovered, I've certain proclivities that others may find distasteful. But you know that I'm more than that.

I'm not a monster. Iris House is just one of many charities and foundations I give generously to. We can continue, but as a couple. It's a wonderful plan, but I must confess this place has worn out its charm and I'm ready to move on. Now, darling—" he waved the gun at her "—we must be going."

The man was insane. How had she not seen this side of him before now? "You need help," she said, trying to appeal to the logical side that had to be in that rotten brain of his somewhere. "If you tell us where Bella is—"

"My patience is wearing thin, my love," Isaac said, his tone getting ugly. "Don't make me do something I'll regret. Now move."

Emma had two choices. Go with him and quite possibly die or scream and hope Dillon could get to her before Isaac shot her. Either way…death was imminent.

But perhaps if she went with him he would take her to Bella. "Promise me you'll take me to Bella," she said, lifting her chin, forcing an image of strength before her knees went out on her and destroyed the whole effect.

"Of course," he snapped. "Let's *go.*"

Dillon listened from the hallway as sweat trickled down his temple. Isaac West was in the house with Emma.

And Dillon was without his gun.

Stealth and the element of surprise were his only advantages, but as he surveyed the situation, that didn't seem like enough. Since West came to Emma instead of waiting for her to come to him, that must mean that the house the agents were raiding at that moment was the right one. And hopefully Bella was there. He had to believe that was the case, because right now, he had to focus on Emma. Slowly pulling his cell phone, he texted a quick message to Sanford, hoping he got it in time to radio the uniform outside.

He followed the voices outside and slid into the shadows. The uniform stepped into view, his gun trained on Isaac West.

"What is this?" West bluffed, acting affronted. "My good man, put away that gun before I blow a hole in this beautiful lady. You don't want that on your conscience. Imagine the nightmares you'll have, reliving the moment each time you close your eyes. Trust me, you don't have what it takes to weather that kind of hell every night. Do yourself a favor and let us keep walking."

"I can't do that, sir. Please put down your weapon," the uniform responded with a subtle shake to his voice. Dillon swore silently. The uniform was probably fresh out of the academy, assigned to a job his superiors thought was going to be a glorified babysitting gig. Gun or no, Dillon was going to have to take his chances.

Dillon surveyed his surroundings to find the best vantage point and moved into position. He was directly behind West. There was a good chance he was going to get shot. But he was willing to take the risk.

With a short prayer of desperation, he sprang behind West, shoving Emma to the ground before tackling West. A bullet grazed his arm and seared a path of pain across his shoulder, but he had his hands full with West as he struggled with the man. The uniform seemed frozen to the spot until Dillon grunted, "Get Emma out of here!" Then he rushed to Emma's side and pulled her to safety.

Time to end this, you bloody bastard. Dillon reared back and punched West in the face, bloodying his nose and possibly breaking the orbital bones in his eyes. Although the man seemed subdued, Dillon wasn't taking chances and punched him again. Grabbing the semiconscious man by the collar he said in a harsh tone, "That was for Charlotte and Ursula and all the other girls you butchered." Then he leaned in closer and whispered for West's ears alone, "And if you'd laid a hand on Emma…you'd be dead right now."

West gurgled what sounded like laughter and Dillon had to restrain himself. Perhaps it was a good thing he didn't have his gun, because right now, he had an itchy trigger finger. "Officer," he called out. "Come cuff this piece of shit and put him in the car."

The uniform rushed over and did as Dillon instructed, his young face pale in the moonlight. Jerking West to his feet, the man looked to Dillon. "Thanks. I kinda froze," he admitted shamefully, gesturing to the wound seeping blood from Dillon's shoulder. "And I didn't mean to shoot at you. I'll radio for EMS."

Dillon waved away his thanks and the offer. "It happens, kid. We all have those moments we wish we could do over differently. Don't let it eat at you. Now put that POS away before he stinks up the place."

"You got it." The officer pushed West to the car and locked him in. Dillon knew he'd radio for backup. He turned to Emma; she had shock written all over her face.

"It was Isaac West," she said numbly. "I never imagined… I'd hoped we were wrong. I thought he was such a good man. Now I don't know what to believe about anyone."

Dillon knew that feeling. Going to her, he said, "Let's go inside and see about that tea. Tea and a biscuit does wonders for the disposition."

She nodded, but he could tell she was on autopilot. He just hoped to God Bella was okay. Otherwise, he didn't know if Emma would come out of this funk.

Chapter 22

Emma cupped her tea mug and let the warmth seep into her bones, but her teeth had started to chatter nonetheless. Dillon had responded wordlessly by draping a blanket around her. "You're in a bit of shock, love. It'll pass but we should keep you warm. I could call the ambulance if you like."

She shook her head. "I'm f-fine."

Was it over? She looked to Dillon. "Any word on Bella?"

"Not yet. Give it a few more minutes," he instructed softly.

She nodded and sipped her tea, not really tasting the blend but thankful for something to do aside from cry. Another thought came to her. "Are my parents all right?"

"I'm assuming because I haven't heard otherwise. But let's focus on one crisis at a time." In perfect timing his cell phone trilled and he answered immediately. Emma held her breath, not quite sure if she was ready to hear the verdict.

Dillon looked grave, his mouth setting in a tight line. Her eyes started to water of their own accord, and she began to shake her head against the news she didn't want to hear. Dillon hung up and he drew a deep breath before coming to her.

"No," she breathed, the tears flowing harder. "She's not dead. She's not. Tell me she's okay. Dillon," she wailed, clutching at his shirt. "Tell me she's okay."

"She's alive," Dillon answered, his eyes fierce. "She's in the hospital. She was hurt pretty bad. It looks like she fought her attacker."

Bella. She sagged against Dillon and heaved a ragged sob that was part relief and part horror, but even as she wanted to collapse, she forced herself to stand and wipe her eyes. "Let's go," she said, her voice weak and a bit wild. "I have to see her."

"Of course," he agreed, and she wanted to kiss him. So she did. Pulling him to her, she sealed her mouth to his even as the salt from her tears dried on her cheeks. "Thank you," she whispered against his lips. "Thank you, Dillon McIntyre. I love you with everything I have and always will."

She didn't give him a chance to respond. She was already leaving him behind, anxious to get to the hospital.

While Emma sat with Bella in recovery, Dillon got the rundown from Sanford.

"Man, that kid's one tough cookie. She fought hard. He beat her pretty badly," Sanford said in a low tone in the hospital waiting room. "I didn't think she was going to make it but she's a fighter. Her testimony will go a long way toward putting away that sick freak."

Sanford gave Dillon a sidewise glance. "I couldn't have closed this case without your help," he said. "Hell, it was mostly your case anyway. I just sewed up the loose ends.

Either way, I'm just glad this psycho is off the streets. I have a feeling he wasn't ever going to stop."

Dillon agreed, the closure felt good but he was bone tired. He and Sanford traded verbal notes for later, but Dillon was ready to find Emma and take her home. He stopped and wondered what that meant, if anything.

He found Emma sitting beside Bella, her hand caressing Bella's even though the teen was still out cold.

"How's she doing?" he asked softly.

"She's pretty out of it because of the painkillers, but she needs her rest." Her eyes welled with tears and she paused to wipe away the moisture. "I'm just so happy she's alive. I can't pretend that she's just a boarder any longer. She's a part of me and even though I'm not old enough to be her mother…I love her as much as I loved my sister."

Dillon nodded, letting the admission rest between them. "So now what?"

She shook her head. "I don't know."

"How about this…let's focus on getting her back on her feet before we try to figure out the heavy stuff. Okay?" he suggested, and she agreed with a soft nod. "How about we come back in the morning? You could use a rest."

She looked ready to protest, but as he held his hand out to her, something seemed to click within her and she didn't resist. Instead she smoothed Bella's hand with her own and then rose to accept Dillon's.

"We'll come back first thing in the morning, though?" she asked.

"Absolutely."

And he meant it.

Wherever Emma needed to be, was where he wanted to be.

Emma crawled into bed after a long shower, where she and Dillon shared the hot spray yet didn't do much more than hold each other, and she realized as Dillon climbed in beside her, that this felt real and right. She'd thought that after tonight she'd be numb inside, but as Dillon's arms wrapped around her and drew her against him, warmth filled the cold spots in her body and she knew there was no place she'd rather be.

The logical part of her—at least the part that wasn't frazzled and short-circuited—was asking all the questions that seemed important in her life before today. Where was this going? Did they have a future together? What did they really have in common? Would she be able to handle being the girlfriend or wife of an FBI agent? Would he want her to give up Iris House? She'd never even been to his apartment yet she was contemplating a blended life with him.

There were all those questions and more, yet, snuggled up to him, she drowsed in complete satisfaction, succumbing to the soul-deep fatigue that dragged on her eyelids—and she realized all those questions…didn't mean a thing. Somewhere along the way, she'd fallen for an agent who should've been the last thing she needed in her life, but had turned out to be the best.

Everything else would fall into place in its own time. And she was ready to quiet her brain and trust her heart.

Epilogue

Six months later...

Dillon leaned in for a quick kiss as Emma finished the last of the day's work before they could leave for Bella's big day. Today was the day that Bella would move in with her new adoptive parents.

It was a tough one for Emma, but she was brimming with happiness for the girl even if it meant letting go of her in the short term.

"Bella, let's go," Emma called out, surprised her voice didn't crack from the ache in her heart. "We have to get going if we're going to make the airport on time."

"I can't find my lucky necklace," Bella hollered back. "It was just here and now it's gone. Evie! Did you take my heart pendant? I know you were eyeing it last week...."

Emma smiled through a wash of tears. She'd miss this. Truly... She winced as Bella shrieked at Evie as she stomped down the stairs. "I know she has it! That thieving liar!" she huffed, dragging one last suitcase and handing it over to Dillon, who was waiting patiently to put it in the car with the rest of her luggage. "If you see her wearing my necklace—"

"I will put it in the mail and send it to you right away," Emma promised, lifting a wash of hair from Bella's eyes. Since her ordeal, Bella had worked through her aversion to touch. It was backward thinking, but Bella made a bit of a transformation when she emerged from the hospital. It was almost as if she was determined to grab on to life and all it offered. The first thing she did when she was well enough to be moved from ICU was grab Emma and hold on to her.

Emma and Dillon had managed to find a family for the teen, and, after D'Marcus had done a thorough background check, preparations were made to remove Bella from the state's care and relinquish her into that of the Baker family.

Dillon tapped his watch. "Clock's ticking, ladies." Then he disappeared outside.

Emma was getting ready to follow when she noted that Bella had stopped and was staring at the house.

"Anything wrong?" Emma asked, worried.

"I'm going to miss Iris House," she said softly, turning to Emma. "But mostly, I'm going to miss you. Thanks for never giving up on me."

Emma didn't have the words for the emotion spilling over in her heart. She swallowed and nodded, gathering her in a tight hug. "You have to promise to email me every day. I want to know everything about your day, your school, your new parents. I want to hear about it all."

"You will," Bella vowed, breaking the hug to stare at her. "And you have to promise me that you'll let me know when the wedding is because I'm going to be your bridesmaid, right?"

Emma smiled. "I wouldn't have it any other way."

Bella grinned and bounded for the car, looking every inch the teenager she was and should've had the chance to be before life dealt her a crappy hand. It meant the world to Emma that Bella was getting that second chance she deserved, and she had Dillon to thank for it.

She'd since started to allow Chick to take over most of the duties of running Iris House, and while her style was different, donations to the house had doubled, which allowed Emma to sleep at night without worrying about the house's closure. To her amazement, letting go of some of that control had actually been a good thing for everyone. Chick was coming into her own as the director and she was damn good at it, while Emma was learning how to live her life just for herself. It was liberating and not the least bit as scary as she'd feared.

She allowed the love she felt for the two people closest to her to warm her soul. Like Bella, she was learning to embrace life and all it had to offer.

And that life definitely included the sexy Brit who stole her heart when she wasn't looking, filled her life with joy and made her toes curl when the lights went out.

Oh, and the accent didn't hurt, either.

* * * * *

COMING NEXT MONTH

Available December 28, 2010

#1639 COWBOY DEPUTY
Lawmen of Black Rock
Carla Cassidy

#1640 DANGER IN THE DESERT
Code Name: Danger
Merline Lovelace

#1641 THE SHEIK'S LOST PRINCESS
Desert Sons
Linda Conrad

#1642 UNDERGROUND WARRIOR
The Blade Keepers
Evelyn Vaughn

ROMANTIC SUSPENSE

SRSCNM1210

Spotlight on

Classic

Quintessential, modern love stories that are romance at its finest.

See the next page to enjoy a sneak peek from the Harlequin Presents® series.

CATCLASSHPI I

Harlequin Presents® is thrilled to introduce the first installment of an epic tale of passion and drama by **USA TODAY *Bestselling Author Penny Jordan!***

When buttoned-up Giselle first meets the devastatingly handsome Saul Parenti, the heat between them is explosive....

"LET ME GET THIS STRAIGHT. Are you actually suggesting that I would stoop to that kind of game playing?"

Saul came out from behind his desk and walked toward her. Giselle could smell his hot male scent and it was making her dizzy, igniting a low, dull, pulsing ache that was taking over her whole body.

Giselle defended her suspicions. "You don't want me here."

"No," Saul agreed, "I don't."

And then he did what he had sworn he would not do, cursing himself beneath his breath as he reached for her, pulling her fiercely into his arms and kissing her with all the pent-up fury she had aroused in him from the moment he had first seen her.

Giselle certainly *wanted* to resist him. But the hand she raised to push him away developed a will of its own and was sliding along his bare arm beneath the sleeve of his shirt, and the body that should have been arching away from him was instead melting into him.

Beneath the pressure of his kiss he could feel and taste her gasp of undeniable response to him. He wanted to devour her, take her and drive them both until they were equally satiated—even whilst the anger within him that she should make him feel that way roared and burned its resentment of his need.

She was helpless, Giselle recognized, totally unable to withstand the storm lashing at her, able only to cling to the man who was the cause of it and pray that she would survive.

Somewhere else in the building a door banged. The sound exploded into the sensual tension that had enclosed them, driving them apart. Saul's chest was rising and falling as he fought for control; Giselle's whole body was trembling.

Without a word she turned and ran.

Find out what happens when Saul and Giselle succumb to their irresistible desire in

THE RELUCTANT SURRENDER

Available January 2011 from Harlequin Presents®

HPEXP0111

MARGARET WAY

Wealthy Australian, Secret Son

Rohan was Charlotte's shining white knight until he disappeared—before she had the chance to tell him she was pregnant.

But when Rohan returns years later as a self-made millionaire, could the blond, blue-eyed little boy and Charlotte's heart keep him from leaving again?

Available January 2011